Edited by Douglas Glover & Maggie Helwig

COMING ATTRACTIONS
93

This book was published with the assistance of the Canada Council, the Ontario Arts Council and others.

Acknowledgements: "To Be There With You" by Gayla Reid was first published in *Malahat* and "Sister Doyle's Men" by Gayla Reid was originally published in *Prism*. "Open Zoo" by Barbara Parkin first appeared in *Descant*.

ISBN 0 88750 928 2 (hardcover)
ISBN 0 88750 929 0 (softcover)

Cover art by Kathy Gillis
Book design by Michael Macklem

Printed in Canada

PUBLISHED IN CANADA BY OBERON PRESS

Introduction

The English novelist John Braine used to divide books he read
into the quick and the dead—and most were of the latter cate-
gory. But the three writers included in this year's *Coming
Attractions* are quick indeed, distinguished from the ruck of
literary-magazine and over-the-transom hopefuls by their
precise delineation of complex emotional and mental states
(what is hidden, what is lost) and their conscious attention to
a fluid yet perspicuous prose style. Eschewing post-modern
pyrotechniques and acts of verbal prestidigitation, they apply
themselves to building, word by word and block by block,
complicated and disturbing objective correlatives of a world
where, to quote Barbara Parkin, "beautiful things are always
being destroyed," a world where a veneer of ordinariness
conceals pain and loss—a boy gone blind and reading
Shakespeare with his fingers, a mother nursing a former lover
crippled in a far-off war, an ageing virgin writing prim letters
to her promiscuous niece and wondering what might have
been.

Gayla Reid came to Canada from Australia in 1967 to do
graduate work and never went home (except in her heart). She
now lives in Burnaby and writes and edits legal material
centred on poverty law. A founding editor of the journal *A
Room of One's Own*, she has already made a respectable contri-
bution to Canadian letters. But now, with her own fiction, she
is charting a new course for us with her stories of love and
random death in distant neo-colonial wars. Her perspective is
Australian, she writes about Australians, but there is something fresh and universal in her approach—reading her, I am
continually saying to myself this is about me, this is about my
family, this is about Canada, too, only no-one has ever written
it before.

Hannah Grant comes from Fredericton but is currently
studying environmental biology at St. Andrews University in
Scotland. Her story "The Forest of Arden," published here for

the first time, has won the New Brunswick Writers Federation Fiction Prize and the Dan Hemingway Prize at St. Andrews. Grant writes in a lushly poetic prose style, weaving whole gardens of theme, imagery and allusion through her pieces. She focuses tightly on the inner mental life of her characters, writing stories that are subjective, lyrical and dream-like (sometimes even hallucinatory) and also wonders of concision as in "Icarus," a marvellously brief retelling of the old Greek myth.

Barbara Parkin was born in Winnipeg but lives in Vancouver where she writes plays as well as stories and is raising a two-year-old son. She writes deft modernist parables akin to Raymond Carver's blue-collar minimalism, stories of sad, frustrated, disappointed people trapped in the coils of domestic situations gone sour, people in doubt and alienated from their own best hopes, ordinary people, decent (though imperfect) people, modern-day heroes. A typical Barbara Parkin story starts discursively, with a deceptive flatness of effect, then suddenly hardens into a tight emotional knot near the end, revealing the dark underside, the agony and deprivation, of our Norman Rockwell lives.

DOUGLAS GLOVER

GAYLA REID

To Be There With You

Water, the smell of brown water, its presence all around. On the one side, the river, meeting the ocean, taking its time. On the other, the South China sea, with its small surf.

I sit in the hotel-room and I wait for Ron.

When I went to that country I took with me one newspaper clipping. It was a photo of a Buddhist monk, who in the protests of the year before had poured gasoline over himself and burned to death.

I pinned it on the wall of the hotel-room, as a challenge. Quickly, it was discoloured by the humidity; it curled at the edges.

The city had by this time become a series of clichés. It was these clichés I sent home, once more. You remember: the pedicabs, the oxcarts, the cyclos, the capricious streams of laneless traffic, the taxi fleet of neurotic blue-and-cream Renaults, the pall of exhaust. The big gutters at the sides of the streets, pungent. The water sellers with their panniers balanced on bamboo sticks across their shoulders, the shoeshine boys, the prostitutes in miniskirts. The bars and massage parlours along Tu Do, the clapped-out tamarinds. The checkpoints, the flaking plaster on the buildings at the heart of town, the hotels—Graham Greene's old Continental and the thin, new Caravelle, where the Australian embassy was located.

I described these things and I looked at the Buddhist monk. And I felt discouraged.

Two things I did not write about:

The people who lived there. What did they talk about when they talked with one another?

The corruption of unknowing. (*Did the people of Vietnam use lanterns of stone?*)

It was a relief to go down to Vung Tau, where the Australian forces were headquartered.

The room I finally found in Vung Tau was everything it should have been. It had vile plumbing and dubious bedding. Everywhere, plants in pots. And tiny wrought-iron balconies that looked out toward the water (you couldn't see it, but you knew it was there). After Saigon, Vung Tau was wonderful.

It was a bit embarrassing, in this French colonial setting, to be happy with Ron. Ron was in the regular army. I should not have approved. It was the men who'd been drafted I felt for— the nashos, the national servicemen, conscripts in a foreign war they knew nothing about.

In my letters home to friends I changed Ron into a French journalist. I had met him, I claimed, in the Saigon offices of La Presse. The only trouble with Henri, I wrote, is that he talks all the time.

One of the best things about being in Vungers was that I didn't have to go to the daily briefings. In Saigon, I was terrified—not of the war, but of the press corps.

There were hundred of accredited correspondents in Saigon; they came from all around the world. There were women among them, some of whom were really famous. They were the ones who scared me the most. With the men, I could excuse myself.

But the women. I trembled.

Every day from about two o'clock onwards, a sinking feeling set in. Around three o'clock I'd decide to skip. From then until shortly before four I'd feel as if a mighty load had been lifted from me. From four onwards, I imagined myself taking part, and wished I were there.

I should be walking along Nguyen Hue to the room above the art gallery. I should be going up the steep stairs, choosing one of the hard, fold-up chairs, preferably near the fan. I should be examining the roneoed sheet that gave the daily statistics.

This was the Vietnamese briefing, and it was usually over within a few minutes. Nobody was interested in what the Vietnamese had to say about the war.

The twenty minutes between 4.40 and 5.00 were the worst. This was when the journalists chatted with one another as they dawdled over to the main event—the briefing at JUSPAO, the Joint US Public Affairs Office, just down the street.

The Free World briefing.

At JUSPAO there was the relief of air conditioning, there was ice water, there were comfortable chairs.

I saw myself with Henri, moving easily among the journalists, handing our passes to the Marine at the door. The two of us, part of the crowd, making our way through the JUSPAO corridors to the auditorium at the back of the building. At the entrance to the auditorium we pick up the daily handouts, and I look to see if there are any Australian ones. I have some quick, perceptive thing to say. Henri laughs. After the briefing we are part of the crowd again, going off to the top floor next door, to eat frozen food flown in from the States. And to complain about it, later.

I should have been there for the show itself, which I did enjoy. First, the chief of the US mission usually came on and made a few remarks. Against the curtained stage, he looked exactly like the master of ceremonies. Then the colonels gave a spiel: ground briefing, air briefing, complete with slides and coloured maps, no expenses spared. They spoke in a dense military argot that I did not understand.

Then came the best bit: the questions. (I never asked a question myself.) Question time often generated a fair bit of snarling.

Once or twice during question time, the entire auditorium would be siezed with something, alert, strained. I didn't know what it was but it felt like the hairs going up on a dog's back.

Atrocities were not yet defined as news. News, at that time, was numbers: 189 Reds die in three battles.

I wrote in my diary: I look at Ron and my bones turn to milk.

Then: no, no, that sounds like dog food.

And later: D.H. was right, but T.E. probably more Ron's man.

I kiss him and my mouth shivers.

Start with what you've got, they'd told me back home. Always get the names of the boys' hometowns. Find out how many sisters and brothers they have, what the father does. See if any of the country papers are buying.

The Singapore-based correspondent who was my main contact described my presence in Vietnam as a "colossal brass-up." He found out about Ron, and said, "Now we'll get some in-depth coverage, nudge nudge."

Each time Ron was coming down from the Dat I was busy all day (clean the room, buy French pastries and bottles of Coke, paint nails—hands and feet, iron clothes, etc.). Ron let me know he simply couldn't get over his good luck: here he'd found someone to be with who wasn't a prostitute. He didn't have to worry about getting the jack.

I washed my hair and imagined Ron, 30 kilometres away, having his shower. Getting clean for me, safely back from the bush. Again.

I was the only woman he'd ever slept with besides Shirl. So he said, and I believed him. He was shocked by the prosti-tutes; a lot of the soldiers were, especially the ones who used them. (They were a pretty straight-laced bunch, the Aussie soldiers.)

There were women and children fighting them. They couldn't get over it.

While I wait for Ron, I look at myself in the mirror.

I love you, I say to the mirror, to Ron, who is not yet here.

Is this how love feels?

Vung Tau juts out into the sea like a small boot.

In the crowded front beach area there is a persistent feeling of holiday. Lots of Aussies, steady boozers all, and Yanks on their in-country R&R. There are the Koreans, and there are the South Vietnamese themselves. And moving among them, invisible, are the VC. For nobody denies that the VC, too, routinely use Vung Tau for their own R&R.

On the front beach evenings begin early, with a kind of nervy gaiety. By night's end that has deteriorated into something thick and heavy and tangled. You can smell the beer soaking into the dirt. You are forced to listen to the song declaring, with a hideous, accurate sentimentality, that the carnival is over.

On the back beaches the soldiers settled in, and were kept busy protecting their equipment from the sand.

Vung Tau was easy to write about: details piled up without effort. I visited the orphanage the soldiers were restoring in a nearby village; I interviewed the surgical team at Le Loi Hospital; I wrote abnout Villa 44, the rest and convalescence centre; I mentioned the Grand, the main watering hole. The town, I claimed, had "a crumbling French ambience." The young Vietnamese women in their *ao dais* "seemed to float along the boulevard." That gave me particular pleasure, using the word, "boulevard." Me, a kid from Australia.

I produced these lying, partial stories and at first I was happy enought to do so. I believed I was getting somewhere. I wrote the way the soldiers wrote letters home. Only they knew what they were censoring, and I did not.

Once that fact became clear to me, I became preoccupied with it.

Back home, it was a Liberal Prime Minister who said, "You are right to be where you are and we are right to be there with you." They wanted to suck up to the Yanks.

But I liked the soldiers. They were nice and ordinary and

scared. I knew what their homes were like on Saturday after-noon: a radio would be blaring the races. If they were Sydney boys, I knew what football teams they cheered for, what beaches they went to.

How they'd eat fruitcake and drink beer on a hot December afternoon.

What mum would cook for tea and where she'd hang her apron, how mum had made that apron herself and trimmed it with a bit of rickrack.

What sort of tin Nanna kept her biscuits in. What kind of biscuits they'd be, how they'd taste.

It was just as well I knew something about the soldiers, I reassured myself. Because they told me nothing. Nothing at all.

I am up at the lines at Nui Dat. I am talking to men just back from the bush. I stand in front of them in my miniskirt, with my long young legs. I ask them to tell me about the war.

Before Ron, I'd had one other lover, and considered myself experienced. With him, love had been an overwhelming project, constructed out of words. I would rehearse the words, analyze and revise them, finding them ill-suited to the huge task.

With Ron there was silence. His body understood. We could sit in two separate chairs and feel whatever it was, humming back and forth.

Because the soldiers told me nothing, I had to make do with geography.

Leaving Nui Dat, one sees the red soils of the dry rolling hills with their rubber, banana and coffee plantations give way to a brief flowering of tender green paddies that are, as we approach Vung Tau, suddenly usurped by the salt marshes and mangroves in their drab Army colours.

I tried again.

Nui Dat, which means "small hills," is actually located in a rubber plantation, I chirruped. Above the camp one sees the Nui Thi Vai, the mountains that the soldiers have dubbed the Warbies, after the Warburtons in the state of Victoria.

I even managed quotes: "Conditions are fair enough, really. You don't expect the Ritz."

We had been lovers in a past life, I decided. In some smoky Celtic cottage, in a valley full of mild rain, I had waited quietly for him.

Even in that life, he'd been married.

There wasn't any question of my mucking things up with Shirl.

I am sitting with Ron in the courtyard of the hotel at Vung Tau. We are reading the Sydney Morning Herald.

Ron is reading what some of the Labor politicians are saying about the war. He looks cranky. Ron's been a Labor man all his life.

I am reading the review section. It is quoting famous writers on the US involvement in Vietnam. (There's a new book out.) I like the Pinter quote: "They were wrong to go in, but they did. Now they should get out, but they won't."

Might come in handy some day, I think. I copy it into my diary.

"What's that you're writing?" Ron asks.

"Nothing," I say. "Nothing."

What does he do out there in the war? I picture him: he is in a VC village. He takes a grenade from his body, pulls the pin out, and chucks it down the well. (Is that what they do? They do use a hand grenade for something like this, don't they?)

I can see him walking away, through the village, away from the ruined well. He has now grown very tall; he walks in giant boots.

These images come to me when I am moving my hands over his body.

I wonder if Shirl reads my pieces. Shirl is sitting in her kitchen, in the Sydney suburb of Bexley North. Her kitchen smells of white toast and Vegemite and kids. The neighbours are proud of Shirl, coping on her own with the two kiddies. Shirl is proud of Ron, her soldier, her man.

It is, after all, no more than a year since the Battle of Long Tan. And at Long Tan we won by 245 to 18. We Australians excel at outdoor activities of all kinds.

I dream of writing something like that, especially for Shirl.

Everyone had a camera; cameras were all the rage. There was this photo of Ron and me and his best mate Johnno. We are in the courtyard of the hotel at Vungers. Ron has his arms around my shoulders. Johnno is beside him, holding up a beer, putting on the big bronzed ANZAC act. Ron is looking at me, sort of smiling.

I swear, if you had seen that photo, you would have said he loved me.

At first it seemed that there was Ron with me and the war on one side, and Shirl and the kids back home on the other. As the weeks went by it felt different. On the one hand there was Shirl at home and me in Vungers. On the other hand, there was the war. At this rate, I told myself, I'd never be *bao chi*, a proper journalist.

Beer left Ron as tightlipped as ever, so I got my hands on some Thai grass. Ron agreed to give it a go.

It made him completely paralytic. He sat rooted to his chair, unable to move. From time to time he said, "Ratshit, mate. Ratshit."

It was a profound truth. But I was no further ahead.

Sometimes after sex he did get a tiny bit talkative. Like this:

"We were going down this bloody hill and we walked straight into the noggies. Right on top of them."

"And, and?" I urged.

15

"Felt a bit sorry for them really. Poor bastards. Having their smoko."

"I love you," I say to Ron.

Ron was older than the man I'd been with before and his big heavy body pressed down upon me without apology.

(Do I love him, do I, really?)

Having been brought up Catholic I believe in the power words can have, particularly when repeated.

"I love you Ron."

He gives a short, tight laugh.

Being there, I am forced to consider the camouflage of language: how much, in the attempt to conceal, is revealed. At the briefings, the favoured line was, "Contact was made." Not even, "We/they made contact."

I listen to what Ron says about the Yanks. They were a piss-poor lot, really. Went crashing around like a mob of bulls in a china shop. Sat on their backsides waiting for Sunday dinner to be flown in. Cranberry bloody sauce, mate, in the middle of the jungle. Translated: Ron liked the Yanks; he liked their clumsy bigness. He was happy enough, in his own way, to be there with them.

There was a South Vietnamese military training centre in Vung Tau. Some of the kids there, I decided, must be highly disciplined cadre from the other side.

I considered the phrase, highly disciplined cadre. It suggested a staggering confidence of belief.

In Saigon—this was before Tet—one could pretend that the Vietnamese you came in contact with were pro-US (pro us). In Vungers you just knew it wasn't true. Here were Vietnamese people serving you food, washing your under-wear. Just down the road was Hoa Long. And Hoa Long was VC by night and had been for years.

In Vung Tau I thought about that more: a double life.

16

It is raining. We are in the hotel-room. Since Ron was here last, his best mate Johnno has been killed by a mine.

Ron stares out at the balcony. He is smoking. He says: "We'd just come out into the rubber. It was lighter, in the rubber."

He says: "Bits of him. Hanging from the trees."

He has never said anything this explicit before.

I look at his grey face, his hunched shoulders.

I go over to him, kiss him, press my breasts against his back. After a while, he is lying down and I am moving on top of him. I feel, as I am doing this, that I have become someone completely ancient.

A woman is pushing her soft body against a man's, trying to make war go away. She is powerful. And ambitious. And definitely pleased with herself.

We'd start off drinking at the Grand, then go on to those makeshift places that had sprung up along the beachfront— little round huts, they were. I'd try to get Ron and the others to talk about the war. What about Dak To? (Dak To was where the main US fighting was going on.)

What about it? They spoke of the cricket scores back home.

Sometimes in one of these bars you saw a soldier crying his eyes out. "Ratshit," his mates would say. Then look away.

We are in a bar. It's not long since Ron's best mate Johnno.

A chap called Ian comes up. He's young and he's really handsome. Ian starts slapping Ron on the back, in a familiar way that is part friendly, part hostile. "Zip 'em right down the middle, mate," Ian says. "Whaddya say mate? Zip 'em right down the midle."

He's very drunk.

"Beauty mate," Ian goes on. "One for you and one for me."

Ron, who's quite a bit older, says, "Take it easy mate. Just take it easy, eh."

But Ian keeps on keeping on.

"One for you and one for me. What do you say? Ripper, mate."

Ron gets up and punches him in the stomach, hard.

That shuts him up.

I didn't see it as any big deal—Ron's punching him. They were all pretty physical guys.

What interested me was what Ian had said.

I'd heard it before.

After the drinking and fucking had been pushed to the limit, and Ron was almost asleep, out of it, he'd mumble, under his breath but loud enough for me to hear: "One for you and one for me."

He could have been back home coaxing his kids to eat up their peas.

But I didn't think so.

Hair brushed, perfume fresh, I open the door, expecting Ron. We are going to the Beachcomber to eat hamburgers and drink that weak Yank beer.

It isn't Ron. It is some other soldier I know vaguely. Awkward, not looking at me.

A tunnel, he says. Ron went down the tunnel. Then he says something about what kind of bunker system it was.

I think, quite without anger: the technical details are so terribly important to all of them; why is that?

What was he doing down a tunnel? Wouldn't he be way too big?

Three column inches on the front page of the Sydney Morning Herald. Australian Task Force troops...Operation Dingo...Phuoc Tuy province.

At home, the neighbours will be coming to Shirl's door, carrying food.

Shirl opens the door and the neighbours come in and sit down in the lounge room, feeling slightly elevated, on stage.

Shirl is holding up like a trooper. Shirl's the widow.
  She has that.

The soldier took me drinking. Some of Ron's mates gathered
round.
  "Good bloke, Ron," they said. "Good bloke." And drifted
off.
  They were pissed and miserable and it was just one of those
things. They did not, they did not, any of them, say it had been
worthwhile.
  I walked back to the hotel and the night moved like water.
  I had been looking forward to the weight of Ron, upon me.

Sister Doyle's Men

In this photograph my mother is on horseback. Behind her, there is a row of hills. Gums are tossing in the wind. (They look like gums, anyway.) The horse has its head turned sharply. I suspect she is holding the reins too tightly.

This is, as my mother's handwriting on the back of the picture says, "Somewhere in New Guinea."

At one corner of the photograph you can see the shadow of the person who is holding the camera. You can make out the shape of the hat. It's a slouch hat, pinned up on one side.

"Who's that?" I ask my mother, pointing to the shadow.

There is a slight pause. Then she says, "One of the men."

My mother is wearing trousers and a shirt. It is wartime.

My mother grew up in Sydney's eastern suburbs. "Where on earth did you learn to ride?" I ask her.

"You learned," she says. "You learned fast. All sorts of things."

It is a black-and-white photo, of course, but the contrast is sharp. "The hills look very green," I say.

My mother looks at the photo again. "I was green all right," she says. She laughs. "You can say that again. I'd only been there three-and-a-half months when that was taken."

I wondered why she mentioned the months, and so precisely.

My mother was a sergeant in the AAMWS, the women's wing of the Australian Army Medical Service.

My father was in the Seventh Division. My father was a Rat at Tobruk.

When Australia's Prime Minister Curtin brought the Seventh home my father was promptly sent to New Guinea, where he was involved in the fighting around Lae.

My father told no war stories, kept no war souvenirs. (Unless, as my brother says, you want to count Mum.) But my mother spoke of the war often, which, given her work, was not surprising.

"He brought them home," she'd say, of Curtin. "He was determined that Australia would not go. He gave those Poms what for, he did."

When I was a child I thought everybody knew about the Seventh, how the Prime Minister brought them home.

My mother met my father in Moresby. They got married right away. Six months later, I was born.

As adolescents, my brother and I consider this story. I am horrified. (What if the nuns find out?) My brother, on the other hand, is much impressed. "The sly old goat," he says. "You've got to give it to him."

"What was she like when you first met?" I ask my father.

He says the usual things: good looker, always one for a laugh.

"No," I say, "what was she like, really?"

I should know better.

"Oh, things were at sixes and sevens in those days," my father says.

My father is one of those old-style Australians who guards his personal life with a wildly unwarranted tenacity. My father gives nothing away.

My mother's secrets are safe with him.

Why did she choose my father? My brother and I decided it was because he had come through unscathed. Both in the Middle East and in New Guinea my father was what he calls one lucky bastard. My mother knew she was going to need one undamaged man in her life.

For somewhere in the green hills of New Guinea, my mother became acquainted with death. Despite her seamless, unspoiled husband, despite the clamour of her two children, she did not return to the house of the living, not completely.

My mother was Sister Doyle.

Sister Doyle was in charge of the ward in Rhodes Repat. where they kept the men who had been wounded in the war and who would never recover. Those men, still breathing but in essential ways already dead, were her life.

For a child in my mother's house, certain appearances on that ward are mandatory.

There is the Christmas party, held in mid-December. We sing "away in a manger, no crib for a bed." We pass out gifts: magazines, books, lollies, cigarettes. These last for those who still have lips with which to suck, to smoke.

There is the afternoon of Christmas Day itself. We go from bed to bed with trays of fruitcake, with glasses of port and Scotch with straws in them. We take our presents to show the men.

We are not the only children summoned to Sister Doyle's ward. Her men are to have music, the sounds of children, singing.

The Catholic kids sing "God Bless Our Lovely Morning Land." The state school kids sing "Old King Cole" and (in possibly dubious taste) "I Am a Happy Wanderer." The choirs do not go right into the ward, as we do. They stand at the milder end. If they are lucky they do not even notice the odd small lumps further down the ward. They do not see the beds at the far end.

These beds have mysterious hoops in places where faces usually are.

Adults come, too, to entertain. On New Year's Eve the local pipe band comes to pipe out the old and in the new. They march up and down the ward, these pipers. But they are grown up. They know when and where not to look.

The Scout Master comes to our house with money from the bottle drive.

"That will go toward a very fine Easter hamper, and I know

you know how much it means to the men," my mother tells him, appreciative. He blushes.

They all come—the Rotary blokes, the Lions, the Masons, the St. Vincent de Paul—my mother makes no sectarian distinctions. This is the early fifties and they wear the little Returned Services League badges in their lapels.

They are, all of them, returned men.

I learned that phrase naturally, without thinking. Later it seemed to typify the to-hell-and-back theme—which had great currency at that time. For the men on the ward, who did not really return, it seemed especially fraught.

When my mother sits with the returned men in the lounge-room, they tell war stories. These stories are exceptionally vague, innocent, featureless.

Here's one: There was this anti-aircraft gunner in Darwin. Name of Bluey. Anyhow, Bluey, he had this sulphur-crested cockatoo. When the air-raid siren went, the cocky said: "Time to get under the sink, Blue."

I did not understand why they found this amusing. But how they laughed.

Conversation grows a little more interesting when there are other nurses there. They talk about the tents they used as operating-theatres. "Oh, the mud," my mother says. "Oh, the stench," the other nurses say, happily.

If I were asked to construct a portait of somebody in my mother's position at that time, I would certainly make her a monarchist, a believer in religion and a conservative in politics. But my mother was, curiously, none of these things.

She saw religion as having its uses, however. She favoured Anglican funerals. "They give the best send-off," she said. "The flowers of the field."

Her interests in politics cut off at 1945. She was not in any sense a cold-war warrior and in that embodiment of fifties stodge, Australia's Prime Minister Menzies, took no interest one way or another. The fifties, for my mother, meant Korea. And Korea meant two new men on the ward. My mother worried they wouldn't fit in. They were younger.

As a young adult I would say that my mother was, at heart, the universal soldier. (And she really was to blame.)

There was this man on the ward, Teddy. He'd been in my father's unit. Came from the bush, out Walgett way. Used to ride in all the shows before the war, my father said. A crack shot, too, was Teddy.

That was how my father met my mother—Stan had gone to the hospital in Moresby, looking for his mate Teddy.

Teddy could not move. His spine was a write-off. He couldn't speak, either. He could move his eyes from side to side and that was about it. Teddy got totally messed up in New Guinea. Over the years Teddy improved, gradually, until he could manage to talk a little. To the outside it was just gobble-gobble, but Sister Doyle could decipher every word.

This is what Teddy said: "I'm in this and I'm doing the best I can."

When my mother liked someone, when she considered them to be her friend, she'd tell them about Teddy. When she repeated what Teddy said, she never used the third person. She always adopted the first person:

"I'm in this and I'm doing the best I can."

"How's Teddy?" my father would ask my mother.

"He's a battler, is Teddy," my mother would say. And her voice would be full of something heavy, like love.

I think now of how Stan met her when he went to Moresby.

She walked down the corridor toward him, listening to the floorboards creak, her stomach in a knot. (Outside, through the louvres, the green hills.)

He figured it out soon enough, he realized how things stood with her. And his face barely moved a muscle.

That would have reassured my mother, she would have decided then.

On Christmas Day, when I am eight, this happens:

We are in the ward, and I am sitting at a window. It is a quarter to five, the end of the afternoon.

Earlier, we were all here, my father and brother as well. My brother got a cocker spaniel puppy for Christmas, named Queenie—this is the Coronation year. A boy should have a dog, my mother says. Queenie was brought in to show the men.

Now my father has taken Queenie and my brother home. My father and my brother are already besotted with Queenie. They take turns carrying her with excited tenderness.

The men, those who could reach out, felt Queenie's soft round head, stroked her ears. Those who could see looked into her brown eyes. Queenie was a big success.

Around tea-time there was a full-blown high summer thunderstorm. (My mother hurried to the men who whimpered.) Then the furious rain. Now, it is over and the ward is filled with a peculiar golden light. My mother has thrown open the windows and the smell of rain rinsing through the hot earth, the smell of fallen gum leaves fragrantly rotting, fills the room.

My mother is sitting on a chair between two of the beds, and everything is calm. She has brought her men through the fracturing demands of Christmas Day, with its forced cheer. She has given them her children, and Queenie. She has stood by them in the thunderstorm, and now she has for them this coolness, this relief.

I look at my mother and with a piercing clarity, I see how she is resolute and obsessed. And I am her daughter. As she is, so I will become.

I am suffused with this fact; I am magnified—not by joy but by a terrible certitude. And I am really very frightened.

I look away from my mother. I inspect my presents from the other nurses. My favourite is a wooden pencil box. It has two storeys. You swing out part of the top layer and there is a secret second layer, beneath. I slide my finger into the farthest recesses of the pencil box, in that second layer, beneath the place for the rubber. I plan what I will put there.

It is so quiet I can hear the clock ticking at the end of the ward, near the entrance. Instead of numbers it has the words, *Lest We Forget*. The small hand is on the second E, the big hand has just passed the G.

My mother was always so busy that it took me a long time to realize what her main burden was: the slow grinding of time, its absolute refusal to pass.

Sister Doyle knows all their birthdays. A good six weeks before the birthday of Shorty or Curly or Jacko (they keep their boyish wartime nicknames) my mother writes to his family. In recalcitrant cases, she telephones. Trunks please, she asks, her voice serious. I wish to place a trunk call.

As you know, she says when the call goes through, Shorty/Curly/Jacko has his birthday coming up. Can we be expecting a parcel? As you know, he's quite fond of Capstans/Winning Post Chocolates/Pix or Post. And it has been some time, let me see, three years, hasn't it? I'd just like to let you know how very welcome you'd be, if it were possible. At all possible.

The parcels arrive—from Dubbo, from Grafton, from Condobolin—drawn by the strength of my mother's will. Sometimes the people come, too.

Apart from the holidays, Christmas, New Year, Easter, there is—of course—the big day itself, the one day of the year: Anzac Day.

My mother knows which division each of her men was in. She has the ward decorated with the appropriate emblems and colours and mascots. Radios are laid on, and, in later years, television sets. Nobody is to miss out on the dawn service and the march. In the afternoon, there is rum and Bonox.

So they inch forward, Sister Doyle's men.

At the end of the road, there is the funeral. And if only a handful of inattentive relatives can be rounded up (thank God that's over), there is the inexpensive solemnity of the last post. And there is, from the priest or minister, these words: They gave their lives. For that public gift they received a praise that never ages and a tomb most glorious—not so much the tomb in which they lie, but that in which their fame survives, to be remembered forever, when occasion comes for word or deed.

I'm not sure where that comes from. It's something I absorbed from my mother, much as other daughters learn to sew a frock or bake a cake.

My mother is never completely off duty. We are walking down to Central to catch the train. My mother points out to us—my brother and me—the plaque on the overpass at the Chalmers Street end: Past this point marched THE MEN WHO WENT. In Martin Place, at the cenotaph, we are not permitted to giggle and fool around. If there are wreaths—and there often are—we are to read them quietly, and with respect.

At school I learn how the Spartans put their children out to die. That reminds me of my mother. If we disgraced her on the ward, I tell my brother, she would put us out to die.

She would be capable of it.

I am making my mother seem formidable. She was that, indeed, but in many ways she was a permissive parent.

My brother and I are allowed to have comics, and she never checks to see if we are doing our homework. A lot of the time she isn't there. She's at work. It is my father who is nominaly in charge.

My father, the unscathed survivor, came home from the war and got a job as a clerk at the lotteries office. At five sharp he takes the train home and retreats to his shed. In the shed he keeps all his carpentry tools, his workbench and his radio. He also has two old lounge chairs (it's a good sized shed). In one of these chairs he sits and smokes his pipe. The other one is for Queenie, and us kids when we come to watch.

My father builds things.

In the fifties my father undertakes two projects that see him through the decade. First, he puts a second storey on the house. This is a posh, unusual thing to do in the ordinary Sydney suburb of West Ryde. Then he builds a whole bunch of built-in furniture. Built-in furniture, in highly lacquered wood, is the very latest thing.

My brother and I each acquire rooms of our own on the top floor, with windows that look out on the ironbark. In my bedroom my father builds a dressing-table that has a bookcase in one side. I can put my hand out and select a book without even getting out of bed.

In the kitchen he constructs a breakfast nook: a round pink Laminex table, with a high banquette, just like in a restaurant. But his *tour de force* is in the lounge-room. There, a combined china cabinet-sideboard-radiogram dominates one wall, a triumph in blond wood.

It is an extraordinary home. It could look like something out of *House and Gardens*, only my mother doesn't complete the effect. In my bedroom I have some second-hand curtains she picked up at the hospital fête.

My brother's friends love the house. Not for its furniture, but because it is always in turmoil. Constantly, one room or another is uninhabitable, owing to the construction work.

My mother is not in the least put out by this. Quite the contrary. "We'll just have to make do," she declares, and her voice is girlish and gay.

The kitchen is in an uproar and my brother's friends are staying to tea. My mother takes the toaster into the lounge-room. We have toast and sardines and listen to *Pick-a-Box*.

"The money or the box?" asks Jack Davey.

"The box, the box," the boys shout, their eyes shining, eager for whatever life will throw at them.

They are always around, the visiting boys. There is the marvellous chaos and what's more, the place is reliably provisioned. My mother goes to cakeshops and buys lamingtons, sponges, biscuits.

This is a shady thing to do, in the fifties—store-bought cakes are looked down upon. "I simply don't have time," my mother says firmly.

My brother's friends help themselves to the rest of the lamingtons and watch my father working. When they've eaten those they can get some Minties from the shed. My father keeps boxes of Minties down there. Minties have cartoons on the side of the box: a fisherman has just reeled in a pair of ladies' corsets.

I don't get in the boys' way. (They're just little kids, really, so boring.) I'm upstairs, staring out at the ironbark.

I'm reading books about girls' schools with no nuns.

I'm looking in the women's magazines, examining the Meds ads. No belts, no pads, no pins. No odour.

My father, Stan Doyle, had been brought up in a Catholic orphanage. He had left school after sixth class and had learned, as my mother put it, "to turn his hand to anything." Had we lived in the bush, Stan would have turned his hand to sheep and cattle. In the desert, he'd have known exactly where to find water.

That a man of manifold skills was putting in his days at the lotteries office was never remarked upon.

After the orphanage, Stan was caught up in the depression, and after the depression he went to the war. Yet Stan is a calm man, sweet and peaceable. A man to turn to in time of crisis.

My mother had to sign papers to say she'd have the kids brought up Catholic. And sign she did.

Off I went to the nuns. When it comes time for my brother to go to school, my mother puts her foot down. He could go for religious instruction. He could make his first communion and all that baloney. But he was to attend the state school and get a real education.

"The nuns are good enough for girls but they won't do for boys," my mother says.

Stan doesn't argue. He isn't an arguing man. But it makes him nervous, I can tell.

Without ever putting it in words, Stan lets me know precisely what he thinks of nuns and priests: a dangerous, slightly loony lot, but powerful. Best to keep on their good side.

Hard lessons, from his own childhood.

At Sunday mass, my father sidles in just before the end of the sermon and sits, ill at ease, near the door—poised for easy and early escape. He looks just like one of those dumb kids at the back of the classroom.

I am the only one in my class who comes from a "mixed marriage." The nuns know.

Whose family isn't saying the daily rosary?

I have to put up my hand.

On the way home from school we exchange insults with the state school kids.

Catholics, Catholics
Eat snails and frogs.

We reply with the more esoteric:

Proddies, Proddies
Fall off logs.

In this way I learn that one side needs the other, even for the completion of a rhyme.

Sometimes in these roaming bands of state-school kids I see my brother's friends. My brother himself.

I wait for the question: "Isn't that your *brother?*"

We are driving over to my aunt's house. We are in the Holden. As we approach the house we can see all the cars, already lined up.

"The football team's out in force," says my mother, signalling disapproval. Her sister's husband comes from a vast family. They dominate these gatherings with a beery, self-congratulatory clannishness.

My aunt, unlike my mother, leads an ordinary life. She stays home. She makes elaborate desserts: rice pudding and jelly layered in tall clear glasses.

I wish my mother would learn to do things like that.

"How's the house going?" my aunt asks my father. He is a fool, her tone proclaims, to squander all that upon my mother, who has not eyes with which to see.

"Stan's got a real showplace," my aunt tells one of the football team. "It could be a real showplace, you know," she says to my mother. (If only you were prepared to pull your weight.)

"Humm," says mother, bored. "What a delicious dessert. I don't know how you do it. Really I don't."

But when we drive home my mother is in a good mood. The visit to the relatives is behind her, one more time. "That wasn't too bad," she says. "Wasn't too bad, Stan, was it?" She's stuck it out and now it's over. She can get on with things. She can get back to the ward.

I look out the window of the Holden and see our ridiculous, extravagant house poking up above all the others. I know we are not a normal family.

We are weird.

My father, who had no childhood family, isn't much of a patriarch. You could say he never developed the knack. But we learn from him, my brother and I. We sit in the old lounge chair in the shed, chewing on Minties and playing with Queenie, and, without even knowing what we are doing, find out how to use a padsaw, a mitre block.

With my father, I have no quarrel.

It's a different story when it comes to my mother. There are scenes.

In this particular scene we are fighting, my mother and me. We are shouting at each other, we are choking out sobs and insults.

Just as Anzac Day is a big day on the ward, it is a big day in our family life. Each year, my father gets out his medals and goes to the march. Each year, my brother and I go with him, to watch and wave and pick him out and feel important. At the end of the march, a photographer takes our picture: my father, my brother and me, standing together in Martin Place. In early years, there were always street photographers on hand. In later years my father takes his own camera and asks one of his mates "to do the honours." When the picture is developed, it stands on the mantleshelf in the lounge-room, where it stays until the new one takes its place.

In this way (I wrote in my diary) our lives are measured out in Anzac Days (three exclamation marks).

This year I'm refusing to go.

I've been to see the play, *The One Day of the Year*. This play— which was, I am convinced, written especially with me in mind—portrays a young man exposing our celebrations, our observances.

Anzac Day turns out to be so much drunken jingoism.

I came out of the Palace Theatre and vomited into the rubbish bin at Town Hall station.

So I won't go to the march, and what's more...

"This place is a madhouse," I tell my mother. "You've been ramming it down our throats all our lives. It's crazy. It's sick. I have a life to get on with, in case you haven't noticed."

"The war happened," my mother says, sharply.

"You could at least stop glorifying the bloody thing," I return.

"I do not," she declares, offended to her soul, "I do not *glorify* anything."

"You do, you do," I reply, going for the upper registers. "You do, you rub our noses in it."

"I do not glorify anything," she repeats (I have really scored, there). "Except courage, courage in the face of pain and loss and despair."

This is as close as I ever come to hearing my mother's apologia for her work.

I flee to the shed, to enlist my father's support.

"You have to stop her," I inform him. "Show her."

He is quiet and mild and he exasperates the hell out of me. "Show her what?" he asks, refusing to be drawn in.

"You're both hopeless," I shout. "The pair of you."

Around this time my mother has a big row with my brother, too. About Teddy.

My brother and I joke about Teddy, but most secretly. It is utter blasphemy. My brother is keen on gymnastics, and practises every evening. He stands on his head and says, for our mutual pleasure: "I'm in this and I'm doing the best I can."

We laugh and he tries his best to keep from toppling over.

My mother catches him at it. She chases him through the house, trying to grab him and hit him. He speeds out on to the road and my mother—to my surprise—does not pursue him. Instead she sits down in the breakfast nook and begins to cry, in a hoarse, windy kind of way.

"You kids don't care about anyone except yourselves, do you," she says. In her voice I hear the beginning of an appeal. I leave the room in a hurry.

Eventually my brother creeps back into the house. For about three weeks my mother treats him as if he doesn't exist.

My brother and I hold whispered, mutinous meetings in my room. We brim with righteous solidarity.

"She should never have taken us to the ward when we were just little kids," I say. "Doesn't she realize we were *scared*?"

"Dad's just as bad," my brother says.

"He just lets her rip," I agree.

Even as we speak we can hear him. He is hammering away on the stairs, replacing a baluster.

One day my mother comes home early from work. This is a shocking thing, without precedent. I'm at home because it's a big feast day—the Feast of the Assumption—and the nuns have given us the day off.

The nuns are always giving us the day off, or so my brother says. It's a wonder you ever learn anything, he says.

I go downstairs to find out what's going on. Is she sick?

She takes her hat off and puts it on the kitchen table.

"Teddy's gone," she says. "Teddy. He begged for it," she says. "For ages and ages. Nothing else. Just that. After all these years. I had to give him what he wanted, you know. I had to." Her voice sounds automatic. (Does she know who she's speaking to? Does she even know she's speaking?)

She takes a chair and goes outside to the back patio that my father built a few years ago. She's still got her overcoat on. It is the kind of grey, still day you get once or twice in Sydney during August. A low day.

She's there at a quarter to six when my father gets home. He takes her a rug and a cup of tea. She pushes away the rug and ignores the tea.

She sits out there in the dark.

My father goes out again, this time to persuade her to come in. I can see him talking to her and I can see her not even turning her head.

He comes back in and he's got a funny kind of embarrassed look on his face, as if he's been caught doing something foolish.

"Let's have beans on toast, eh?" he says.

I make the toast, my brother puts the jug on. My father lights the gas and gets the beans going. We huddle together in the breakfast nook, the three of us, and Queenie.

At last she does come in. My brother and I are in my room. We are supposed to be asleep by this time. She goes up the stairs and into their bedroom. My brother and I creep along the hallway and listen for voices.

Nothing.

What did he say to her?

What did she, finally, say to him?

It is the late sixties and my mother has cancer. She is in Rhodes Repat., so she is, in her own way, at home.

They are fooling about trying to decide which parts of her to cut out. "I've told them to get on with it," my mother says. "Chop, chop." My mother has a nurse's cheery crudity about such things.

Now, of all times, she isn't going to let her men down. She calls for a wheelchair. "They've seen tons of people in their dressing-gowns," she says. "Might as well see me."

Off she goes to the ward. I wonder if it distresses the men, to have her growing thinner and more determined by the day.

By this time there is another war, about which I have come to hold passionate views. (It has given me a glimpse of what my life might be, what I might become.)

My days and nights are full of organizing against the war. Our country's involvement in this war has to end, the war itself has to end. So many other things have to change, and fundamentally. There is everything to be done. I go about in a state of euphoric fatigue.

These visits to the hospital are really very difficult to fit in. It takes two bus rides and a change of trains just to get here. And I have vital work to do.

In my mother's presence I scrupulously avoid all mention of the war.

She's the one who brings it up.

"I was reading in the Herald," she says, "they can bring boys home now that they wouldn't have been able to before." She says this in a puzzled voice. "They can get them out so quickly, and the know-how is so much better."

How can the Vietnam boys (the MEN WHO WENT) be worse off than the men on the ward and still be alive?

She looks to me—to *me*—for an answer.

My brother has been conscripted, but has disappeared into Western Australia instead. Wisely, he does not write.

Officials knock on the door. Plainclothes men, and, on one occasion, the military police. They come to the house. They come to my flat in Bondi.

With my father they are polite. With me, contemptuous, hostile.

No, he's not here. No, I'm not expecting him. No, I don't know where he is. No, no, no.

When my mother is dying, when she is rambling, out of it on morphine, and there is no more question of her ever getting up and going anywhere, she calls out their names: Curly, Joey, Teddy, Blue, Jacko, Stan, Teddy, Shorty, Rusty, Teddy.

With the endless need of the child, I listen for my name, and for my brother's. She does not call them.

My father is left alone in the big empty house.

These days Stan lives with my brother. When I go back to New South Wales, I stay with them.

My brother, who runs an orchard on the Murrumbidgee, has an old-fashioned home with big verandahs. At the weekends the place is often filled with friends (the visiting boys).

At the back of the house Stan has built what he calls a grandpa flat. There's a small workshop down there. Although he is now in his eighties, he is making for my brother a desk out of stunning dark Tasmanian sassafras.

"Lovely, lovely," my brother says, stroking the wood with his hand and looking in his father's face.

"It'll see me out," Stan says, of the grandpa flat.

My brother writes to me, he keeps me up-to-date.

We were sorting through some old snaps the other day—my brother wrote—and we came across a really early one of Mum—in her nurse's uniform, on what looked like a troopship.

Both arms around some strange young man, a soldier. And smiling. Smiling to beat the band.

"Where did that one come from?" my brother asks Stan, "I don't remember ever seeing that one before."

"Oh, that'd be Teddy's," Stan says, easily. "Used to carry it everywhere with him."

"Teddy's?" says my brother.

"Teddy's," Stan says.

"Used to carry it everywhere with him?" my brother says.

"That'd be right, I reckon," Stan says slowly, evasive now. "Before. Before he. You know. Got messed up."

Then—my brother wrote—the old coot gets up and pours himself a cup of tea. Stares off into the middle distance, as if bored.

When I come home they drive up to Sydney to meet me: Stan, my brother and his wife.

We go to visit my mother's grave.

She has a small bronze plaque. The rising sun of the Australian Infantry Forces is in the top right-hand corner.

I put my arm through Stan's. I look over at my brother.

Stan looks down at the grave, at Sister Doyle's name.

I don't say anything.

Stan lifts his bony face, sniffing the air. He turns to my brother.

He says: "When I get completely buggered I'll go down the back paddock and you can shoot me."

"Oh Dad," says my brother's wife. "You mustn't talk like that, not when we love you so. It isn't right."

Father Kenny

On a Friday morning in November, as I wrote the last exam of the year at uni, my father, 50 miles away, drove the ute out on to the highway and was sideswiped by a semi-trailer. He spent most of the summer months in the local hospital, where he was visited regularly by the new parish priest, Father Kenny McCready. It was across my father's bed that I met Kenny, at the beginning of the long vac.

Or rather, met him again.

Father Kenny was no stranger to our family. He and my brother, Anthony, had been at Springwood and Manly together. Boys of the same diocese, they were ordained in St. Mary's Cathedral. At the time of their ordination—a windy spring day—I was in Fourth Year at the Angeline Convent and the school choir was on hand to sing the mass. Anthony and the other ordinands prostrated themselves full-length before the altar. They were wearing those long white things they call albs. They were said to be priests forever, in the order of Melchizedek.

The families were out in force. My father was there, and my Aunt Dorothy. That was it for the Careys.

But the McCreadys! Piles of them. They filled up their appointed rows. They overflowed.

The new priests bless the members of their families. It is a damp-eyed moment, a tremendous reversal of power. We Careys were up and blessed and back in our seats, but the McCreadys kept coming. Two of the McCready clan were the Sullivan brothers, who played Rugby League for New South Wales. We had seen their pictures in the paper.

The Kenny McCready who faced me across my father's bed had been a priest for four years. Like his cousins, he was a good footballer. The Young Catholic Workers approved. The older women of the parish approved of him too, as such women do approve of men who are beginning to fill out, men who are young enough to be their sons and who are now striding confidently along in the world.

"Everyone loves young Father McCready," my Aunt Dorothy reported. She was using the word "loves" in a general sense. Also, perhaps, the word "young."

That summer Kenny was 32 years old.

I am sitting by my father's bed. My father, at this stage of his illness, cannot speak. He is on oxygen. But he can hear. The nurses show me how to converse.

"MR CAREY! HOW ARE YER GOING? ALL RIGHT? LOOKING GOOD TODAY!"

My father can press hands quite coherently and can, in fact, hear without being shouted at.

"Hello Dad." A hard press. "I'm putting the calves up and milking Jess." Press. "The chooks are all right." Press. So it goes, the two days a week I spend at the hospital.

John Peters, our neighbour who is taking care of the property, drives to town on Tuesdays and Thursdays. The ute was a write-off in the accident. I could take my bicycle but it's fifteen miles, half of it gravel.

After I pick up some groceries I go to the hospital for the rest of the day. My father and I listen to the test cricket on the radio. I read him the scores from the Herald. I read him the trivia from Column 8. I read him the local news from the Northern Daily Leader.

The priest drives me home.

With him, I discuss my courses at uni (Old and Middle English, Latin, Philosophy); Anthony's successes (studying in Rome, he is); the property (John Peters is fixing the fence by the creek, John Peters is going to sew down the pasture). The cricket. The drought. The Kennedy assassination.

On the day of their ordination, they had their pictures taken, all the new priests, standing together in the cathedral grounds. When I look for that picture among my father's things, I find it without any trouble. There is Anthony and there, standing next to Trevor Millane, is Kenny McCready. They look dazed, dazzled. They would have just come off the long retreat that preceded ordination. It was their day, at last. It had happened. *Father* Anthony. My father had blinked and said, "...if only your mother."

Of course I know that nothing can happen between me and Kenny McCready. First there is the obvious. Secondly—a distant second—I am supposed to be going with someone else, a man called Malcolm Travers.

Malcolm Travers was a graduate student in Chemistry but he liked to hang around the English Department and take part in the play readings it put on. Travers was a good reader and could make people laugh. I remember him in *Waiting for Godot*, chucking turnips around. And in a play by Christopher Fry, getting a good response to the line, "always fornicate between clean sheets."

Travers was a married man.

I should have been mixing with those boring Newman Society types. But I wasn't.

My time with Travers was spent in his Austin, parked on one of the back roads behind the uni. Travers had an English wife and an infant kid. The wife was unhappy about her new country and disorganized about the kid. Nappies everywhere, Travers said. Kid yowling. Wife in tears. Liquid pouring from every orifice, he added, warming to his theme. Tears, milk, blood, shit.

Disapproving of any newcomer who whinged about Australia (Poms, especially) I pressed myself against him, to make up for it. The windows of the Austin fogged up.

I thought that he wouldn't be willing to put up with me for long, being a married man. Yet to my puzzlement he persisted.

When I met Kenny my preoccupation with Travers flew out the window, leaving behind nothing stronger than surprise. How could I be capable of such fickleness? I did not have the kind of face I believed one would need for such a thing. My face is long; I thought of myself as looking like a horse.

I studied that face in the mirror. *O fals Cresseid*. It was not Chaucer's but Henryson's Cresseid I had in mind. She comes to a bad end, that one, *sonkin into cair*.

Kenny has slowed down for the cattle grid. He takes his hand off the gear shift and places it on my right thigh. We bump across the grid. He puts his hand back on the steering-wheel. The car moves on.

All summer long I am alone in the house. My father is in hospital. Anthony is at the Gregorium in Rome. My mother is dead. Aunt Dorothy drives out from town regularly, to see how I'm getting along; she always comes on Sunday afternoons. Peters is often on the property, but he rides over the back way, from his own land, and is rarely at the house.

Behind the box gums by the woodheap my father's dogs slouch about (men out of work). At the sound of Kenny's car they bark and pull on their chains in wild distraction. Later, when he goes, their barks diminish only after the last beams of the headlights have swept away in the darkness.

So nobody comes: we have the place to ourselves.

I feed Kenny baked custard and stewed fruit, Big Sister fruit-cake. He plays the 78s my mother had bought when we got the electricity hooked up. He opens the piano, plays a few notes, groans, and settles in to play some more. Since my mother's death when I was thirteen nobody has played the piano much; none of us has the talent for it.

Kenny can play by ear, a fact I find marvellous, extraordinary.

The early hours of the evening are a busy time. People are in their homes with their children. They are listening to the radio. (Some even have TV.) They are dumping the tea leaves in the back garden. If there are no functions at which he is expected, nobody misses the parish priest.

He never leaves later than 8.30 or a quarter to nine. Drives back into town, back to the presbytery. And no-one knows.

Or so I think.

Kenny had clear and definite plans about how we should be together, what we should do. I concluded that men were like that. Later, when I had other men as lovers, I found myself waiting for them to orchestrate particular, formal gestures, and was confused to find them random, casually opportunistic. It took me some time to put my finger on the possible difference: when it came to planning, Kenny had had at least twenty years.

He took the eiderdown off my father's bed and laid it down in the orchard, beneath the greengage plums, among the sheep droppings.

I want to look at you, he said.

And afterwards, to look with me, up through the leaves to the sky, where the stars were coming out.

He danced with me to my mother's records. His chest was bare and I was wearing my best skirt. He held me solemnly.

These stagey activities unnerved me. We are in the orchard scene, I thought. We are in the dancing scene.

I fortified myself with port, a sophistication recently acquired at uni.

Kenny got the atlas out and showed me how we would drive over to Broken Hill, then down to Adelaide, across to Perth, and up to Geraldton. Imagine, he said. The Indian Ocean.

Together we looked at the map. The impossibly distant, *Indian* Ocean.

A child of the fifties, I came to love-making with the expectation that it would be apocalyptic. It had been surrounded with such dense, promising secrecy. Lawrence, one of the few who had anything explicit to say on the subject, said it in extravagant metaphors everyone seemed to take seriously.

I looked at Kenny's body. I looked and I touched and I felt, and there were many small ridges and hollows.

This is what religion is about, I decided. *This* is his body.

The way in which the items on the mantelshelf could grow dim and fade away seemed to me a powerful revelation. There is the Toby jug, a wedding present to my parents. There is the picture of my mother holding Anthony with one arm, and bracing herself on the verandah railing with the other. Anthony's shawl hangs in a luxuriant sweep and my mother looks down, devoted. In another photo I am three years old, on the beach at Coogee. Further along the mantelshelf there is a cheap little china giraffe, which I bought years ago as a Mother's Day gift. All of these items move into a static clarity. Finally—and I watch this happening, I wait for it—they recede. They are wiped out.

Afterwards, the plates clack against each other as I take them down from the cupboard. The knife, sliding through the fruit cake, is met with a satisfying resistance. The cake slides on to the white plate and sits there, magnificently solid, a central dark rectangle.

I develop a name for it. Quotidian happiness. I look the adjective up in the dictionary, to make sure it's what I want. It's what I want all right. If Kenny and I...we could have quotidian happiness. I believe I already do have it with him. Even the gate to the orchard closes with its own, excellent creak.

One evening Kenny sat down at the piano and played and sang. I recognized the song from St. Patrick's Day concerts: "Down by the Sally Gardens." "She bid me take love easy," Kenny sang, "as the grass grows on the weirs. But I was young and foolish, and now am full of tears."

I knew I would have to pay.

I am sitting by my father's bed and Kenny has not come.

My father is not making the recovery that has been

expected and there is talk of sending him down to the Royal
Prince Alfred, to see what can be done. I cannot hear Kenny's
footsteps in the hall and he does not stand there, filling the
doorway. Instead, the nurse has come to announce that visiting hours are over. I am being thrown out. I have to get up and
walk over to the door, down the corridor, down the steps and
out into the street.

I must set my face in place. The jaw. Think about keeping
the jaw sitting quietly beneath the teeth. Breathe. Remember
to breathe.

In the Middle English I had studied lovers fell *doun in
swoun*. I had laughed. I had not known, then, that they were
describing a physical fact.

Walk along; I am walking along. I am walking home alone
because he did not come. I will have to walk all the way home.
Fifteen miles.

Listen to the cicadas, singing. Singing of dust and summer
and seven years in the ground. At St. Angela's the chapel
smelled of cool stone and candles; then the incense. *Adoremus
in aeternum*, we sang. I shall love you for ever and ever. Outside,
the cicadas sang that soon we would be breaking up for the
summer holidays. We wouldn't have to get up at six o'clock
every morning. We could eat all the biscuits and lollies we
wanted. We were going home.

Here is John Peters and he is asking me if I want a lift. John
Peters, innocuous as his name, does not ask questions. Does
not say, how come the priest isn't driving you home? How
come the priest—that priest of yours—didn't show up today?
John Peters is a silent, rural man and thank God for that. John
Peters, held up today at the ram sales, is that mildest kind of
believer, a four-wheeler Anglican (baptisms, weddings and
funerals). Wouldn't know what all the fuss was about.

How would it be like to be John Peters? What would it be
like not to have to worry? I put my arm on the window: casual,
normal. Tell him about the Royal Prince Alfred; any day now.
My father. Not what they expected.

In the gorges to the east there were bushfires. The sun went over in a haze and Kenny did not come. In the orchard the apricots ripened and fell. The lorikeets carried on like a bunch of drunks. After a week I took a bath. I washed my hair. I ate.

I lit the copper and took down the curtains and washed them. They had not been washed since my mother's death and some of them fell apart in my hands. I fished out the survivors. I rinsed, dried, starched and ironed them. Those I could not wash I hung on the clothesline and poked at with a broom.

I put the blankets in the bathtub and jumped up and down on them. I cleaned the silver. When I went to town with John Peters I bought varnish and did the hallway and the lounge room, where the carpets didn't reach. My mother had been a determined woman—witness the way she had kept Anthony's name intact—and she had washed and shone as if it were a language she was fluent in. What a falling off there had been over the seven years! Stains on the tablecloths, and, in the cracks between the lino, a steady accretion.

There was a lot to get on with.

My Aunt Dorothy, pleased to see I was keeping busy, said it was high time I left uni for good. The place was packed with Protestants and atheists who refused to wash. I should come home and take care of my father, who needed me. It was what my mother would have wanted, she said. (I think the housework really got her hopes up.)

What my father wanted, I countered, was for her to move out from town to take care of things. After I'd gone back to uni, I added hastily. With my aunt I felt loose and wild and bitter. And, for the first time, powerful.

So Aunt Dorothy, who had put in ten years with her bedridden mother (that was the phrase we always used, bedridden) came out to the property to do it all over again for my father. Who in time recovered, and carried on.

Back I went to university.

And no letter came.

I ran into Travers in the student union.

"Haven't got the plague, you know," he said. "Where've you been?"

No, I thought, it is I who am the leper. But I will not repent.

What have they done with him? What has happened? Have they punished and shamed him?

Does he despise me for what I did? Does he pray for forgiveness? Forgiveness for me?

Well I wasn't sorry. Not in the least.

If only he would write!

Was he really not going to write to me? Not *ever*?

My one satisfaction was that I could tell Travers I had met someone who made fooling around in the Austin fatuous.

But Travers was a changed man. His wife's stitches had healed up. Everything was back in working order, he was happy to report. Up and running smoothly. And the baby. The baby was sitting up and looking around taking everything in, a curious little monkey.

"You really should see the baby," he said, rhetorically. "Really, you should."

So. He was not going to ask and I was not going to be able to say no. I was to be denied even this one thing.

I stomped off.

Kenny was waiting to contact me. One day he would show up and I would leave whatever I was doing, leave immediately. I would leave the ink still wet on the page and the coffee warm in its mug. We would drive to Broken Hill, to Adelaide, to Perth, then up to Geraldton, and nobody would bother us, nobody would know where we were, who we were. He could get a job teaching Latin. He might show up in need of clothes. I had one of Anthony's old sweaters. It would do in a pinch. The black trousers wouldn't be too noticeable.

When I came back from lectures, he'd be there in the parking-lot, waiting for me. He'd be tapping at my window at three in the morning, sounding like the wind. I would hide him in my room. (He could use a bucket.)

It would be like the French resistance. I would smuggle him safely out.

Home for the May holidays, I went to work on Aunt Dorothy. Turned way from her, arranging groceries in the cupboard, I asked her about the new parish priest.

"Old parish priest, you mean," she said.

Father Mulchay was back, and he was much better now, he was his old self again.

Mulchay hit the grog, everyone knew it.

I was forced to push on.

"What happened to, you know, Father McCready?"

"I couldn't say for sure." Pause. But she had heard something, come to mention it. He'd been transferred to another diocese, was it Grafton or Maitland? Yes, down to the Maitland diocese, that was it.

The following September, she had some more news. A friends of hers had been talking to Father Mulchay—his problem had come back again—and she said that he said that Father McCready had not been well. Not at all well. Bit of a breakdown in fact.

Where was he?

She didn't know. If I was so keen to find out, Aunt Dorothy said, I could go to mass on Sunday for a change and ask Father Mulchay myself. It was all very well and good over the Christmas holidays when I was out here on my own without a car. I was excused. But now here she was, with the Holden, and there was nothing to stop me from going. What my mother would have said, she didn't know. And hated to think.

They had driven him crazy and locked him up somewhere.

They would do it. This was the mob that brought you *strappado*.

Why had he let himself be locked up in a loony bin? I knew what went on in places like Callan Park: they put them in the cold showers and beat them with broom handles. It had all come out in the Sunday papers.

Maybe they had a place like that, especially for priests. Did they make him practise mortification of the flesh? In the twentieth century, today, Jesuits still whipped themselves, and a lot of others did, too. They kept this nice and quiet, but they did it, just the same.

It was in this state of mind that I completed my degree. I became one of those drab young women who stand at the edge of things, who can't scrounge up anyone to go out with them, not even to the college ball.

I listened to what the others said about this one and that one: why doesn't he phone, he just didn't tell me, what am I going to say to my parents? When they sat in the common-room in tears, needing to be comforted with cups of tea, I felt a sour vindication.

Weekends were the worst. They closed the library at lunchtime on Saturday. Whoever heard of any self-respecting university library that wasn't open on Sunday?

Because he neither wrote nor came, and for want of anything else to do, I studied and did quite well. Well enough, in fact, to get a scholarship to go overseas, to graduate school.

They asked, "What were you doing when Kennedy was assassinated?" And I did not answer, truthfully, "I was asleep." Instead, I said, "I was falling in love with a priest." When this went down rather splendidly, I amended it to, "I was in bed with a priest." But the success of having had something smart to say turned out to be not what I'd been looking for, after all. It was the particulars I was interested in. Kenny and me. Me and my Kenny McCrea.

With my new lover, I was more determined. Did he have any idea what it had meant? The strain? Didn't he *realize*? We were flying in the face of God. No need of mirrors, Kenny and I. We had God the Father, God the Son and God the Holy Ghost getting their almightly knickers in a twist about what was going on.

"Well, move over Copernicus," my young man said. A kind young man, really. Fed up with me. "Give Galileo the news. No, the sun is not a fixed body in the heavens. Lo, it has come to earth and dwells among us, although we know not where. What we do know, my fellow sinners, is that it is shining, shining constantly, out of this Kenny-priest-guy's ass."

It was like that, with me, for a long time.

If it wasn't for my brother, Anthony, I would have lost track of Kenny entirely.

When I came home after years overseas, I went to see Anthony. He was back from Rome and teaching at the Manly seminary.

It seems to me—and this must be a commonplace observation—that the seminary at Manly contrasts sharply with the goings-on below. On the hill, the house of celibacy. In the streets, at least three of the seven deadly sins on daily parade—lust, gluttony, sloth.

This was where Kenny had spent the final years of study for the priesthood. Perhaps it was the bouncing Manly sun and the flash of bodies that first gave him a sense of the possibilities.

My brother strolled with nonchalance among the hedonists in the streets. He sucked on his disgusting pipe and gave me the news. About my father's funeral, which I hadn't come home for. How John Peters bought the property, stock and all, How the house now stands empty and the orchard is going wild.

After family matters, the conversation moved on to more general topics. Trevor Millane, now a monsignor, is secretary to a bishop. Travels a lot. Kenny McCready. "Do you remember him?" Anthony asked. "Oh yes," I said. "I remember him. Ordained with you wasn't he?"

Kenny left the priesthood. Went to America, to Los Angeles. Is doing his doctorate in marine biology at UCLA. They'd lost touch, but Trevor got his address through the family, and wrote to him. Kenny wrote back.

All the time I was in the States, Kenny was there, too. I could have dialled LA information and got his number. Just like that. I could have gone out to the coast on a Greyhound bus. If only I had known.

I would have done it, too. I would have gone out there and made a fool of myself.

The letters to Trevor continue. Kenny is a good correspondent, after all. (I never would have guessed.) During my annual January visits with Anthony I get the occasional update. Kenny is working on his post-doc. Kenny is moving to Oregon in the northern spring.

The peripatetic Trevor goes off to Oregon on a junket with his bishop. Meets Kenny and his wife.

His wife.

Spends an evening with them. No, no children.

What's his wife like? A very pleasant woman, according to Trevor. Canadian. A biologist, also.

Pleasant: agreeable to the mind, feelings or senses. To all these three, one hopes. And does he have quotidian happiness with her?

I was wrong, of course, about the word, "quotidian." Quotidian: a sturdy cargo ship is working its way across the Pacific. Night falls and still the solid thing ploughs on, rusted out but enduring, tough.

There is more. Kenny has broken into print. His book, *Nudibranchs of the North East Pacific*, is for sale in the local bookstores there. Trevor brought some copies back.

"It seems," said Anthony, mildy, "Kenny has given up on God and taken up with slugs instead."

In his introduction Kenny explains that his speciality is nudi-branchs. Pronounced "branks" he tells us.

He thanks "all the brankers up and down the coast."

50

The nudibranchs are described in taxonomist's detail. But Kenny enthuses, too. One nudibranch has a head of deep violet. The oral tentacles are red at the base and distal end. The foot corners and rhinopores are yellow, tipped with white.

"This must be the most beautiful little aeolid on the whole west coast!" Kenny exults.

I don't have a clue what he's talking about.

"These delicate small animals," he goes on "are known as the butterflies of the sea. They astound and delight, simply because they are."

Anthony and I walked along the Corso. My annual visit, again. I told him that my marriage—to the kind young man—was going down the toilet. I used the shallow, ugly phrase deliberately, to keep things at a distance.

And despite all my resolutions I began to weep: familiar, tedious, boring tears. "I'm so fed up with being like this," I said, to my brother.

In the middle of the Corso, Anthony embraced me, held me close. As he did this I was aware of the big sandstone seminary on the hill behind me, the seminarians.

I told him that priests had come a long way. He laughed. He knows what I think of the Church.

"Since when?" he asked. "Since when have we come a long way?"

We went for ice creams in the blue-and-white place with all the clocks. Midnight in New York. That means 9.00 PM on the west coast.

A night of early dark in the middle of winter: Kenny is inside. In his room there are hardwood floors, bookshelves with glass doors, Persian rugs. Kenny is listening to a violin concerto. Bruch, he is listening to the Bruch. He's seated by the fire, which right at this moment flares up with a bright sodium flame.

Outside, where I am, there is the cold smell of dead wet leaves.

I see his pleasant, Canadian wife (a biologist also) come into the room.

Anthony, Trevor and I were sitting at a picnic table on the back verandah of the cottage they now rent each January, for a fortnight's break at the beach. Drinking passable cask wine and picking at the last of the mango-and-passionfruit salad. Talking about nothing much. The king tides, the cyclonic disturbance off the coast.

I was up for the weekend.

It was dark and the mosquitoes were beginning to bite. Anthony brought out a mosquito coil.

When I saw a man wading through the water with a dog, I looked up without much interest.

We could smell the frangipani along the side fence— always stronger at night—and the surf. These two add up to the most romantic smell on earth, Anthony said.

A decade ago I would have picked up on this at once, demanding to know what romance might smell like in heaven, what priests could claim to know about romance. Now I didn't bother.

People paddle across the creek all the time. It's the short cut between the beach and the camping ground. When Anthony looked down at the water, and at the man coming out of the creek and into the back yard, and said, "Oh here's Kenny," I did not connect.

"Kenny and Martha," Trevor added.

I looked at him and all I thought was, "Oh, Martha's the dog." A Master's Voice dog, perky.

I looked again.

Same square face.

Christ, it's him. It's him all right.

Christ, he looks like a wild man from the bush.

Christ, he looks old.

However did he get to be such a grandpa?

Then he came up onto the verandah and Anthony said, "This is my sister" and he nodded and said, "Of course, how are you?"

He sat down at the far end of the picnic table. Anthony and Trevor talked about how wonderful it was to live without TV, not to listen to the news. He agreed.

He said, "I'm out at sea for weeks on end and I don't give a stuff about what's going on in Canberra, or Washington. Or Rome," he said, as an afterthought, nodding to Trevor and Anthony.

"It could be another world," Kenny said.

"It is another world," he added, helping himself to the wine.

He was working on a new book, *Nudibranchs of the South West Pacific*.

Camping across the creek, going out in his boat every day.

Anthony didn't mention it. Didn't occur to him that it might be a news item.

"Nobody tells me anything," I said.

Then Trevor told a story. When the three of them were in the seminary together in Springwood, in the Blue Mountains, they didn't hear a radio for months on end. Seminarians were not supposed to be interested in the things of this world.

During the Suez Crisis Kenny lay on the floor with his ear to the floorboards, trying to hear the radio the priests were listening to in the room below.

"It was enough to give you piles," Trevor said. "Piles of the earhole."

"It wasn't cold at that time of the year," Anthony said.

"Bullshit, mate. It was freezing all year round in the seminary," Trevor said.

After a few more glasses of wine Trevor and Anthony went off to play Scrabble in Latin. They do this only when they're at the beach. Each year, they claim, they remember less and less.

Trevor said, "The grey cells are dropping their bundles."

Anthony said, "We pray to remember."
"*De profundis clamavi ad te Domine,*" Trevor said.
Anthony took it up: "*Domine, exaudi orationem meam.*"
They both laughed, but Kenny didn't.
Had he forgotten the words?

It was different after they'd gone. Kenny slid along the bench to be next to me.

I could smell the smoke from the mosquito coil, mixing in with the frangipani.

He said, "Funny how mozzie coils went out and now they're back in."

"I like them," I said. "I've always liked them."

Kenny reached out his foot to play with Martha's belly.

"What kind of name is Martha anyway?" I said. "For a dog."

"She waits," Kenny said. "On the boat. Every time I come up from a dive she reckons it's a miracle."

I asked if he was still married and and he said more or less, and I asked what more or less meant and he shrugged and said, "How about you?"

I said, "We're going to have to stop meeting like this. Once every 30 years. If we keep this up, next time we'll be dead,"

And Kenny said, "Carked it. We'll have carked it."

"One of us is going to stand the other up," I said. "It will be just like old times."

"Will it be your funeral or mine?" he asked.

I felt his leg against my leg. The warmth of his body.

I watched the mosquito coil: the small hot knob where it burns, the white ash as it falls, the way the smoke curls upwards and then vanishes.

HANNAH GRANT

Shades of Green

When Grandmother died, Norah lost all interest in her own part of the garden. To be fair, it had always been the shadiest, in the corner under the elm. For a brief time in May, while the rest of the garden still pushed yellow fingers through the mat of last year's leaves, the low spring sun had crept through empty branches into a resplendence of crocuses and scillas, hyacinths and daffodils, which swelled and burst into fragrance with the melting snow. In June, after the funeral, the elm had already begun to spread out its green umbrella, and as the days lengthened it became more and more difficult to see anything that was not also green under the thickening canopy.

The elm had decided Norah's particular plot; she had been the most vociferous in its defence. Alexander said its roots sucked the goodness from the edge of his vegetable patch; Kathleen didn't like the dark, sticky leaves, or the beetles that seemed to love its pitted bark. Eric sided with Norah, with a vague plan for a treehouse, but the elm had just begun to grow into the snaky grace of a mature tree, with side branches at once too high and too thin for climbing or building. But the elm stayed, and Norah was given the surrounding ground, which that summer she abandoned. If she had been able to answer the other children, Norah might have said that she was too exhausted to cherish anything exotic or fragile, anything that required individual attention, isolation or a special name. So the weeds grew green and vigorous, in the green shade, over the black earth.

Eric, whose allotment of space was right against the sunny wall of the house, planted nothing but Grandmother's favourite flower. Bright orange, with an edge of yellow and a centre of deep red, the gaillardias had grown in other years as small, bright flames of colour mixed in with the other perennials. Eric's plot blazed up into a wall of fire, a conflagration of

56

blooms like a great sunset painted on living velvet. Kathleen was more conventionally romantic. She edged the flagstone paths of her rock garden with hedges of rosemary, clouds of forget-me-nots and pale lilies. A devout medieval artist could easily have imagined an embassy of angels among those paths, touching earth sprouting with the symbols of mortality. Alexander sacrificed his usual complete commitment to his lettuces, and the best spot in the garden, to cherish a single, special memorial, a botanical wonder.

Grandmother had ordered it herself in February, when the garden had been buried with snow. It had arrived with the ribboned bunches of carnations and sympathy cards, a clump of reddish stems on a convoluted, bulbous root, blotched with muddy water. It came wrapped in three layers of plastic, with warnings in six languages; a seventh language announced its name: *Paeonia pax praeclara*. Alexander dug a hole almost as wide and deep as a grave, and the small red shoots shone in the dark earth like a bull'seye in the very centre of the vegetable garden. By the end of June, the shoots uncurled into the veins of finger-like leaves as shiny as humming-bird feathers, and a hard red bud pushed up like the hilt of a sword.

Meanwhile, under the elm, the weeds grew luxuriantly green. Feathery chickweed crept, soft and thick, apparently rootless, around the furry branches of that succulent weed that bleeds bright yellow when crushed; the round stems of young swamp maple stretched up, each with a ragged pennant of leaves. The ground was covered by the dark tendrils of a weed Father called "creeping Jesus" with thread-like roots that broke only to keep growing. The fence disappeared behind crouching burdocks, and a spreading tangle of wild grape. In the deepest shade, the Solomon Seal loomed in great curved stalks, which budded into waxy droplets like congealed tears. Norah would crawl into this darkest forest of stems, and lie like one of the cats against the earth, in the dim green light, among the beetles, the woodlice and the bird skeletons.

If she had been able to explain, Norah might have told the

other children that she did not have enough words; she had begun to think in another language. It was too tiring, and perhaps ultimately futile to try and translate in the words she had been used to using; everything she said came wrapped round with false connotations, becoming a distortion, or a limitation. Along with this new language, as part of an exhausting, saturating knowledge, had come the realization that somehow, sleep was much closer to life than it was to death. Under the branching crowns of water hemlock, surrounded by breathing leaves, she filled her mind with wordless thoughts, in this cradling maze of dark green.

When July came in with breathless heat, Pamela came home. She had been planting trees out West; the dry weather had stopped everything indefinitely with the threat of forest fires. Pamela herself was burnt brown and thin and strange; she sat out on the verandah in the long afternoons and told stories while she rolled cigarettes. She talked about trips by helicopter out to long stretches of barren earth where she and her partner would stay all day alone, often working shirtless in the sun. They planted the trees in long rows, each hole dug and filled in one compact motion; Pamela said she made an effort to do it carefully, but she had been told only about one in three survived. She showed Norah and Eric a whistle of bright orange plastic, which she wore on a string around her neck. It was supposed to be a signal for emergencies, specifically bear sightings; the sound could be heard eight kilometers away. Pamela let Norah try it, for a split second only, and the resonance seemed to encompass, briefly, all the bones of her skull.

Every evening, while Pamela's smoke trailed into the stifling air, Alexander would spray the garden with huge fans of water, pressing his thumb tightly against the mouth of the hose. The gaillardias grew tough and stocky in the heat, their stems covered with dry hairs, their petals still outstretched and brave with false fire; Kathleen's wilting lilies revived each night, only to droop again the next day against flagstones that shone white in the sun.

In the shade of the elm, the weeds kept growing. Tall grasses reached up between ferns that spread their fronds in overlapping lattices of darkness. Under the cover of this darkness, fleshy creepers swarmed to the very edges of the vegetable patch, extended cautious runners and smothered the rhubarb. Surrounded by stunted lettuces, Grandmother's peony stood still and straight, its dark leaves and single bud appearing unchanged.

As the hot spell continued, Pamela began to go out dancing at night, at a club that was only about a twenty-minute walk into town. She would come back smelling of smoke, humming and swaying through the dark garden, her voice roughened from shouting through the music. When Kathleen asked, Pamela described the multicoloured lights, the red walls and the big central dance floor with a stage for special demonstrations. The stage was backed with mirrors; Pamela said, laughing, that when the professional dancers had left there were always a few people who would go and dance alone in front of the mirrors. Whether they were practising, or showing off, drunk, or preferred their own reflections as partners, Pamela did not know; she had not noticed whether the mirror dancers were always the same each night. As Kathleen was just about to turn sixteen, Pamela promised to take her along to see before she left, if the dry weather did not break sooner.

The garden was changing colour in the heat. The lawn was patched with brown; flowers appeared bleached between yellow-edged leaves, against earth as dry and pale as dust. In Kathleen's plot the bright stones seemed to make up the garden: the faded stems and petals seemed an afterthought. The vegetable garden looked almost as if it were made of stone: dirt disturbed by the evening waterings coated the leaves and dried during the day, so that each plant was a grey carving. The peony, its grey fist still clenched, appeared ever more like a monument. Only under the elm the weeds still flourished, in the living colours of jade and malachite, agate and emerald. Creeping into the very deepest growth, Norah could still find the damp, rotting smell, and the tiny glints of shell and carapace, slug trail and worm cast, which seemed to have deserted the rest of the garden.

One morning a changing wind brought into town all the smoke from one of the forest fires far to the northwest. When Norah woke up the sky was a dark, vivid yellow; everywhere the air smelt of smoke. It was the thick, ambiguous, lung-tearing smoke not only of wood and leaves but of burning garbage; the indefinite, frightening smell of burning houses, of pillage. Kathleen said that for a few moments, she had thought it was the end of the world. No-one in the house was supposed to go outside, but Norah went out for a few minutes to look at the garden. It looked so strange in the yellow light that she could not bear it, so she went in to the others and slept until dusk.

The next day it rained. The water came down in rivers, gouging out patterns in the dusty earth, beating the dust out of the hairy stems of the gaillardias and washing it into clots in the centres of the lettuces. Many plants lost petals or leaves; the ones remaining shone raggedly with moisture, on stems bent in elegant curves by the force of the rain. Under the elm, the mass of weeds appeared like a huge, crouching beast, at once pressed back and invigorated by the water, which continued to drip for a long time from the branches which at first had provided shelter.

The morning after the rain a long chain of ants emerged from the weeds, and crossed between the lettuces to where the peony stood exposed and upright as a sentinel. The ants climbed up the stem, past the outspread leaves to the sword-hilt, now burnished into a green gem. In a matter of hours the facets of the bud were eaten away, to expose a pale, rosy swelling, glistening with formic acid. The stream of ants reversed direction and vanished back under the elm. All after-noon, in the whole sweetness of the wet garden, the flower began, slowly and slowly, to unfold layer after layer of petals, and to fill the darkening air with fragrance.

That night it was decided that Kathleen would go dancing, even though it was too soon, because any day Pamela would be called away. She borrowed a student identification card from a friend, and helped Kathleen to outline her eyes with black and paint her mouth to look older. Norah and Eric watched them leave, Pamela laughing, Kathleen walking carefully and importantly in her black skirt, around the puddles that caught the moon in flashes of silver all down the street.

At the dancing place, the doors opened with a rush of smoke and sweat, perfume and warm breath. Kathleen moved through the throbbing music and voices until she could see the mirrors backing the stage. In the reddish light, she distinguished her own shape from the others as it moved, not yet swaying, to meet her; gradually, as she caught the rhythm, she let that one reflection blur with the others, and all the faces became one face. Her heartbeat quickened, steadied, until it was the beat of the music, and there was one heartbeat, and one face, and she was dancing.

Back at the house, Norah was dreaming. She saw her grandmother standing in an empty wilderness of black earth, which stretched away in all directions under a dark, yellow sky. Her grandmother had Pamela's orange bear whistle and her whole figure was bent over, straining with the effort of blowing it, on and on, but even as Norah was aware of the sound, she could not hear it. She woke up, her head thrilling with imagined noise, her lungs aching with remembered smoke. The air coming in her window was fresh and white with moonlight; when she opened the back door, she could hear bats calling, like in her dream, just on the edge of perception. Norah bolted out into the garden. She ran through Eric's blaze of grief, over Kathleen's garden of stones, past the single great flower that glowed palely like a second moon. She plunged into the darkness under the elm, where the leaves reached out as thick and cool and moist as the hands of welcoming relatives.

The Forest of Arden

Paul was dreaming of a woman standing in a field with a gun. At first she was a small silhouette against a pinkish dawn sky, smudged by dirt on the train window. She grew larger and more distinct; he could see she wore rubber boots and a coat over a loose dress or nightgown. She held the rifle loosely, all her attention apparently focused on something beyond the train or invisible to Paul. As the field and the woman rushed toward him, he tried to determine whether she was actually moving; just before the train brought them parallel, she vanished in a blur of speed and he woke up.

He smelt exhaust in the cool air blowing in from the window; the vibration of the train became the roar of a passing car. Somewhere down the street a child was crying. Faint music from the next room meant that Gabriel was up and working; Paul groped for the bedside clock and guessed seven thirty two or three. Untangling his legs from the sheets, he put his feet on the floor. He no longer considered the extra few minutes of sleepy half-consciousness he had enjoyed as a child, but for a moment he sat on the edge of the bed, rubbing both hands across his face, then stood up and walked out of his room. The hall smelt of beer and laundry soap; he leant against the bathroom doorframe and reached sideways to turn the taps on full. There was no need to hurry; he would have plenty of time to catch the train.

The derailment that blinded Paul in the summer of his eighth birthday happened during his first train ride. Chance placed him in one of the two cars that were severely damaged. After spending the afternoon of the first day in the observation car, and the night with his family, he had finally decided to explore the front of the train. He was caught standing in the aisle, surrounded by strangers, when the wave of force tossed him sideways into a confusion of soft bodies and breaking glass. He remembered a prolonged shriek, and a shock that he could not remember either fading or ending. After that, of course, there was only darkness.

Paul stepped out of the bathroom just as Gabriel's radio erupted into the rest of the apartment, blasting out a Renaissance dance tune. Paul found Gabriel's relationship to music one of his most endearing qualities as a roommate. He produced it naturally or artificially wherever he went: he splashed and sang when washing; talked back to radio and television; cursed and laughed out loud; walked heavily; whistled; hummed. Sometimes he sang in his sleep. Paul could follow Gabriel's every movement through the apartment, calculate his mood, even recognize his voice from the other side of a concert hall.

Just now Gabriel was singing loudly, if incoherently, along with a soft drum rhythm, obscuring both the main recorder and the harpsichord parts. The irregularities of his voice were echoed by the impact of his steps, and Paul kept a prudent distance as he followed the carolling, dancing Gabriel toward the kitchen. He reached the doorframe just as the exaggerated percussion of the finale was punctuated by the creak of the opening refrigerator.

"Hell, there's no milk!"

"Third shelf, behind two jars. Good morning."

Gabriel swore appreciatively. A second, slower tune began trickling in from the hall. Paul found the kettle, filled it and plugged it in; he found a cup, the instant coffee, a spoon, and his chair. He let the music completely erase the echoes of the dream, the melody gradually replacing the almost subliminal memory of the sound of the train.

After the accident, the effects of concussion had swept over him in waves, pulling him in and out of a coma for two days. He had so strongly associated the return of consciousness with the return of vision that later, trying to remember, he found it difficult to distinguish between this time and many of the days following. Once he had learned to identify his waking hours by the hiss of the air conditioner and the pain in his arm, he began to connect sight with his return home. He moved into his family's new house in the city with only the uncertain recollection of a photograph of the front of a building. For several years afterwards, it seemed to him at times that he had never really woken up, and never gone home.

All at once the kettle began to whistle and the telephone rang; a split second later, whistle, recorder and harpsichord were overpowered by an eerie strain of east Indian sitar. From the hall, Gabriel's voice claimed emphatically that he was not at home, while the real Gabriel knocked over his chair and barged across the kitchen, shouting at the telephone. Paul heard the sitar stop in mid-whine, as Gabriel began an energetic monologue in French. After an equally incomprehensible shout of farewell, Paul heard the clatter of the hall closet opening and the front door slamming closed. Gabriel's footsteps on the metal stairwell clanged into silence like distant bells.

Gabriel, a graduate engineer, was now majoring in theatre arts; he had a vast, incompatible collection of acquaintances who appeared periodically and left obscure messages on his answering machine. When Gabriel was out of town, Paul was responsible for filing and selectively passing on these communications; he heard requests for help with surveying problems, demands for better speaking parts in Hamlet and instructions for the use of special effects such as lightning and small explosions. His position as a funnel for this stream of exotic visitors offset the combination of handicap and natural reticence that tended to let him slide into the careful circle of the blind.

Paul's studies in history required a lot of solitary reading, as did his work in the University braille library. Outside of Gabriel's whirlwind of music and arguments, Paul's main solace was his collection of talking books. He would relax his cramped fingers, brew some herb tea, and settle back in a cloud of fragrant steam to listen to King Lear, or a dramatic recital of Beowulf in Old English, or a commentary on

Darwin's The Origin of Species, complete with recordings of bird calls.

Shakespeare was Paul's favourite; he had versions of all the plays and sonnets. He had tried to explain his preference, and finally concluded that in Shakespeare, visual images were always more suggestive than descriptive: King Lear's storm of despair was only peripherally physical; Prospero's island and the forest of Arden were made up of selective associations, deliberate projections of worlds perceived in the mind. For Paul, visual images in all literature were neither meaningless nor completely understandable: some triggered memory, sometimes sight, sometimes emotion; others did not. He found Shakespeare's symbolic landscapes especially comprehensive, and real.

Paul's favourite sonnet was number 130, the one that begins:

My mistress' eyes are nothing like the sun:
Coral is far more red than her lips' red;...

Paul's recording of this particular sonnet affected him to an extraordinary degree. Even more than the poetry, the voice of the reader, like music, seemed to enhance the significance of the words. It was a young woman's voice, slightly nasal but so clear and light as to be almsot sexless; the self-conscious enunciation and mild distortion of the recording made it sound distant. Paul could imagine that he was hearing the woman for whom the sonnet was written, reading it aloud for the first time, her voice blurred by centuries. The sonnet was part of a collection compiled by volunteer readers from the University; the reader of sonnet 130 was not named, and did not appear on the rest of the recording. Paul had made several copies, as he was afraid of wearing out the original an being unable to replace it.

The sonnet had become so familiar that Paul found himself repeating it whenever he was slightly distracted, using it like a chant to measure distance when he was walking. Picking up his cane from the hall closet, he found his way down the stairs and out of the building. Turning left, he passed two lamp-posts:

If snow be white, why then her breasts are dun;
If hairs be wires, black wires grow on her head.

His relaxed mind offered him a brief view of snow-covered fields striped with a dark procession of pylons and connecting lines; the scene seemed to move past him before vanishing back into his memory.

I have seen roses damasked, red and white
But no such roses see I in her cheeks;

An imaginary smell of snow was replaced by the real, sweet scent coming from the flower stalls near the corner.

And in some perfumes is there more delight
Than in the breath that from my mistress reeks.

Paul felt the warm, malodorous rush of air coming up from the subway station, and tapped his stick to find the first step down. He had memorized routes he could travel alone to get to the library and the University; today a friend was going to meet him at the link to the train station, and travel with him to the conference.

Paul was no longer afraid of travelling by train, as repetition of the sightless experience had built up protective layers of routine. He now found it strangely exhilarating: the vibration, the press of people, the throbbing rattle of speed, all built and sustained an emotional tension, and put Paul in a state of undefined expectation. He had discovered that train rides represented a way of reviving his memories. In addition to the dreams, train rides seemed to open up an unused store of associations, provoking vivid flashes of remembered sight. The effect sometimes lasted for several days. Paul had tried to explain the experience to Gabriel, who began referring to Paul's "visions" as results of train "trips."

On the subway, Paul gripped the handle nearest the door; counting stops. He stepped out at the correct platform, inhaling the pervasive underground atmosphere of damp concrete and fighting the usual panic until he heard his friend's voice, and felt a hand on his arm. As they headed for the ticket office, his apprehension suddenly produced the brilliant picture of a crowded station full of colour and movement. Some of the people Paul knew: he saw a ten-year-old friend who was now married, and a neighbour with a dog he used to walk. Paul looked at other, strange faces, and felt a mild unease. He climbed into his seat savouring the image; he lost it as, with a starting jerk, the train began to move.

Paul returned from the conference feeling unhappy. Another student, a math major, had cornered Paul and forced him to discuss the different ways of presenting computerized geometry in braille. Paul had lost interest in all but simple math when he had lost his sight. His pleasure in angles and lines had been purely visual; he could not understand the perspective of someone who had been blind from birth. As an added confusion, while the student was speaking, Paul involuntarily saw in perfect detail the figure of his father, twenty years earlier, as he had appeared trying to help Paul with his homework. As Paul watched helplessly, his father's image flickered and changed: his hair lengthened, then shortened as his skin darkened; his beard disappeared; a checkered shirt became striped, then was hidden under a sweater. Throughout these transformations, the young student's voice spoke as if from behind his father's face, which somehow managed to maintain an expression of earnest concern. Paul arrived back at the apartment with a sense that he had lost something important, and by having it in the first place, had lost something else. For consolation he listened to ten of his favourite sonnets, ending with sonnet 130. Then he decided to go over the messages on the answering-machine.

Gabriel had replaced the sitar with a sixteenth-century dulcimer; a few delicate chords escaped before Paul pressed the correct button. A young woman's voice said clearly "It's me." Paul was paralyzed; realizing he had missed the rest of the message, he rewound the tape. The slightly nasal intonation was unmistakable; Shakespeare's mistress was coming to collect her script at eight o'clock, as promised.

Her name was Emily Leonne; she was a forestry student who liked drama. She arrived still covered with pine needles from an afternoon field trip. When Paul let her in with a kind of horrified wonder, the scents of resin and damp earth poured into the apartment. He thought he had opened the door to a forest. For a moment he found himself looking into a stand of evergreens opposite that first platform, on that first day. A fox appeared at the edge of the tracks, loped neatly across and vanished into the trees.

Fantastically, the first word she spoke was his name. Gabriel must have told her. Her voice was gruffer, more intimate than the recording.

I love to hear her speak, yet well I know
That music hath a far more pleasing sound;

When she agreed to go to a concert with him, Paul nearly drove Gabriel crazy with planning. He traced the route to the auditorium four times, counting blocks, turns, fire hydrants, streetlamps. Then he made himself sick worrying whether she liked baroque music. Gabriel said if she didn't what good was she anyway, and turned the radio up so that the bass thundered like a summer storm. Emily said she liked the concert, and accepted a drink afterwards. After she left, Paul asked Gabriel what she looked like.

"Dark hair with red in it; dark eyes—brown, I think."

Paul remembered the dark sleepers, the red flash of the fox.

I grant I never saw a goddess go;
My mistress, when she walks, treads on the ground.

He was silent, satisfied.

He asked her to another concert; in return, she brought him a pack of embossed cards and taught him to play poker with Gabriel. Paul gave her a necklace of agate, a cool, fluid weight of rounded stones; she arrived the next day with a balsam fir seedling from the nursery, carefully potted.

The first time Emily stayed the night, Paul rememberd briefly as a revelation the red glow of closed eyelids. For the first time in years, he recognized the border between sleep and consciousness, then it faded into unimportance. He listened to Emily's heartbeat until it became a rhythm in a dream, and he watched the shadows of trees passing, mile after mile, until the darkening sky made them indistinguishable.

Emily took Paul to the movies. They sat in the back and she whispered a blow-by-blow description of all the action she thought he was missing. These outings usually degenerated into normal back row foolishness when Emily began telling lies, giggling, and commenting on their neighbours. As they walked out into the cold of the evening and on into the park, (Emily still laughing), Paul felt as if the characters in the film with their choreographed ecstasy, and the other viewers with their cheerful passion, followed and surrounded them with the heady freshness of the new leaves.

Once she made him go to an evening of country dancing; she traced the patterns of each dance for him, and taught him the steps. The other dancers whirled him around with congenial patronage. Paul could not decide whether he enjoyed himself or not; it was like being drunk. That night he dreamt of trying to keep his balance in a crowded corridor, jostled by faceless giants. He woke sweating, his heart beating quickly in time with the music.

One morning Gabriel announced that he was going on tour. He left with a shout, his windbreaker rustling and snapping like the feathers of some huge bird. For a while it seemed to Paul that Gabriel still hovered in the apartment; half-eaten bags of cereal materialized from under cushions and the answering-machine remained strongly vocal. Emily was much quieter than Gabriel, but no less detectable. Used to being untidy, she made an effort not to leave clothes on the floor where Paul might trip over them; as a result, all chairs and tables were carefully draped. Filmy scarves, work gloves, raincoats, all showed where Emily had just been, where she was going, and where she was. Paul felt wonderfully secure, wrapped in this cocoon of reminders. Emily also filled the windowsills with small trees. For Paul, the apartment might have overlooked a vast wilderness; the scent of sun-warmed evergreen pervaded every room.

Emily read to him often. She agreed to tape other readings for him to keep, but only after some persuasion. Emily did not like the way her voice sounded on recordings; she thought it sounded stilted, high-pitched, too childish. Paul had also noticed a difference between the live readings and the recordings. He loved Emily's voice, and the possessive intimacy of listening to her, but he had come to realize that it was still the slightly distant, distorted voice that he found oddly compelling. Almost guiltily, he would take out his recordings and listen to them when she was away.

One day in the fall, Emily left early for a foresters' clinic in the mountains. Paul got up late; he was still surprised by how much he noticed her absence. That evening, before she was due back, in a nostalgic, conspiratorial mood, he decided to listen to sonnet 130. He played the last lines through twice.

And yet, by heaven, I think my love as rare
As any she belied by false compare

Paul reached over to open the window, spruce needles pricking his fingers. The wind which rushed in was cold; it was getting late. He sat back, breathing in the feral, resinous air, and felt vaguely anxious. The forest in his mind floated like a mirage on the other side of the tracks, silent and insubstantial.

When the telephone rang, Paul was so disoriented that it rang three times before he even reached the hall. He heard the answering-machine click on, and the throb of a drum mixed with the thick, green breath of the trees. Gabriel's voice announced his absence. The music paused, a note sounded, and Paul heard Emily's voice, speaking against the noise of many other voices.

It seemed to Paul that he could still feel the resonance of the drum, but the tempo had become faster and steadier. His lungs filled with cold of remembered snow. In his mind's eye he saw the fox, poised on the tracks. Fences began to writhe past him, stained pink by the dawn; trees shredded the sky around him; a flock of silent crows flew toward him at amazing speed. An ocean of white fields swelled up like a great tide, and he saw the woman with the gun. For an instant, the skeleton of an abandoned barn framed the rising sun.

When Emily came in, a few minutes later, she was nearly knocked over as Paul grabbed at her and pressed his lips against her throat. He stumbled; his feet were tangled in long ribbons of tape and the remains of the stereo system. The answering-machine lay sideways on the floor. There did not seem to be a way to tell her how, overwhelmed with visions, his heart pounding in time with the engine, he had suddenly seen his own face as he had last seen it, reflected in the train window. The telephone message sounded distant; the light voice spoke with nervous precision and sexless clarity. He heard the voice of this child, this eight-year-old self, distorted by the resonance of his own skull, saying:

"It won't be long. I'll be home soon."

Icarus

He was less afraid of the dark than he was of the dust. He was afraid of the dark because of what it let him do to the space around him. He could stand in the largest room, and slowly, slowly make the dark and the silence and the walls close in; the room shrank to the size of an alcove, then a closet, then a cupboard, smaller, smaller and smaller, until it closed around him in a layer of dust, and all he could hear was his own heartbeat and his own breathing. He could not imagine a place without dust, just as he could not imagine a place without fear. He breathed dust, and everything seemed made of dust: *red ochre, brown, ivory, sienna, almost-black,* from the pale shards of bones and the stained tatters of cloth, to the wrinkled face and dry hair of his father. His nightmares were dust-coloured; the yellowed horns and teeth of the monster and the flicker of dull red eyes were always just around the corner. There were so many corners.

This was his father's place, this nightmare of dust and passageways and small, empty rooms. He had lived there for as long as he could remember.

The dream of his mother was his own, and it was this he cherished in the smallest, darkest room he could find, where the darkness was almost blue-black, instead of red-black. His mother's eyes had been blue—blue in a world of ochres, and umbers, and red, bull-headed horrors; her hair had been blue-black and shining. He dreamt of being sheltered and enfolded in curtains of this hair, as he crouched in the dark, his eyes open for fear of the red veils of his eyelids.

He knew that it was because of her blue eyes and blue-black hair that she had died. It was he who had found her, finally, after she had run screaming into one of the side passages; screaming for the sky. She had become a part of the place when he found her, curled up and leathery as one of the bats, her hair bone-coloured with dust, her eyes gone. He knew that she could not have kept such precious things, not in such a place. She reminded him of the birds, things so alien to his world that they could not survive in it; he was glad that the monster had not found her.

The monster was real, just as were the bird carcasses that kept him and his father alive. The roars could be heard occasionally, filtered through dozens of walls and corridors, and the distorted footprints were the signs he used to find the feathery remains of the monster's meals. The other ones he tried to avoid, but it was difficult, with so little light and so much dust.

The feathers always intrigued and repelled him; They were so light, so pale and clinging, yet each one had a sheen to it, and a wiry strength. He ran the longest through his fingers as he followed his father through the endless hallways to the workroom.

Only one passage led to the workroom; it was the only room that smelled of something other than dust. It made him want to shout or clap, at the same time the tension it built in him made him want to run frantically, hopelessly back into the tunnels. He never stayed long in the workroom, partly because his father seemed to feel a kind of panic also, and scrabbled in the piles of feathers and bones with a sense of purpose out of place in an eternity of darkness, and silence, and fear.

He would leave his father to search out the hives that bulged from the walls like growths on the maze itself. The smoke from his torch, the grinding hum of the bees and the dry, dusty wax-smell dulled his alertness, until the everpresent fear of being caught unaware drove him back to the workroom.

His father worked deliberately, frowning, in a puddle of red torchlight. He growled to himself, surrounded by picked carcasses, pots of wax, and drifts of feathers. Fanning outwards in a lacework of hollow bones, the wings were slowly taking shape.

He could never quite believe what his father told him of the purpose of the wings, not because he doubted his father's skill (for had he not built their own whole world?), but because flight had little meaning for him. Bats flew, hissing scraps of leather like shades; birds did not fly. Birds were only found in broken heaps, in passageways tainted by the musk and prints of the monster.

They tried on the wings, there in the torchlight. He fanned the dust into choking clouds, and laughed for the first time since his childhood, as his father covered his face with his sleeve.

They practiced with the wings until their arms ached. Time after time they stood in the dark, eyes shut, faces covered, the only sound the whirring of dust and feathers. For hours. Days. Years. The loose feathers were strengthened, or readjusted, or replaced.

And then, all in one moment, it was time, and they scratched and scrabbled and tore at the wall of the workroom. Their panic increased as they heard the noise they were making; they knew the monster would hear. His hand slipped through.

It was blue, blue as his mother's eyes, a brilliant blue eye in the wall of the workroom. Soon the eye was a doorway, and he could see that there were two layers of colour; the eye, blue, clear, achingly bright, and the other, darker, rippling, blue-black and shining, his mother's hair. Suddenly he was desperate, frightened, eager, and he stood in the light in his dusty feathers while his father stared at him. He did not know that all the dust around him had turned to gold, or that his eyes were as blue as his mother's and as the sky.

As he listened to the sound of the sea, he became aware of the sound behind him; the roars and hollow clatter of hooves were getting louder an louder. His father pushed past him with a shout of warning. The sound of a raised voice startled him so much that he lost his balance and toppled, flinging out his arms to hit a floor that was not there. He could not see the walls of this room, or the floor, or the ceiling. In his surprise, he remembered to move his arms; the world stopped moving, and he flew.

It was so big; he wanted to scream with laughter at how big it was. So he climbed higher and higher, until he looked back down behind him, at his world, the one his father had built. It was a nothing, a brown beehive, a waxy growth of dust. He flew higher and the world he was in grew bigger. Now he could see the small, complicated pile of pebbles and twigs that was the castle, and the green puddle of the royal park. Green was almost as beautiful as blue, and the room grew bigger and bigger. He could see the spread of his father's wings below and to the side of him. His father was a bundle of bones and feathers and twiggy limbs, a piece of the world they had left behind; banking and rising, his white hair flew in dry wisps about his face; his mouth was working. He heard his father cry out in a voice torn to shreds by the wind. He was too used to whispering to shout back, so he smiled his amazement, and climbed higher.

He kept expecting to see the walls, and was fiercely delighted by the way his view expanded as he rose. He could see a large length of coastline, more forest, more ocean...a small dark line on the horizon, far to his left...A pair of seagulls flew underneath him, crying out at him. His father was calling out too, but it was as faint and as meaningless as the gulls. He flew higher.

It seemed to him that there was so much air that it hurt to breathe, and his chest burned. It was so bright, and so clear, and so blue. He watched the world get larger and larger, straining to prove that indeed, there were no walls. He did not notice the increasing flexibility of his wings, or his own uneven strokes.

The wax gave way, the hollow bones snapped, and he fell. In a whirlwind of broken bones and feathers he plummeted, with a shrill cry like a hawk. He shrieked not for fear of falling, for there was no floor to fall to, but out of pure rage as his horizons shortened. The far line of land disappeared; he could no longer see the inland forests; the coastline shortened, narrowed, and vanished. The circle of his view shrank until all he could see was a circle of blue-black, rippling water; first the size of a lake, then a pond, then a turbulent pool. The circle became smaller, smaller, and smaller, and closed around him in a shining curtain of his mother's hair.

BARBARA PARKIN

In Place of You

An ink pad sits on the Queen Anne desk her father gave her before he died. Anne-Therese rolls the date stamp carefully, exacting the correct year, month and day, and when she's certain that all the numbers are aligned, she grinds the stamp into the pad and slams the date onto a sheet of writing paper in a quick one-two motion.

She writes:

Dear Colleen & Keegan

But crosses out baby Keegan's name. Better that than include the father's. She puts the pen down and thinks of what she can possibly say.

Across the room, a blue box sits under the china cabinet. She has seen it there waiting for three weeks. The City Engineering department delivered the box along with a pamphlet detailing instructions on dividing plastics, stacking newsprint, washing cans, and removing their labels and lids. The instructions don't indicate how to remove the gummy labels from glass jars, only that it should be done.

She is afraid of the box. Her niece, the one she is writing, would not understand this. Unlikely, unmarried Colleen—now tucked at home in a little cottage on a Gulf Island, nesting with her baby and some man, apparently Danish and completely unknown to the family—would chastise her for her resistance to the box.

Colleen and her games: still trying on princess' shoes, then a pauper's pair, slipping in and out of political groups, flavours of the month, degree programs, universities, derelict cars, four different addresses in one year, always between jobs, scant men, men's beds.

Poor Colleen. How she needed the hand of a real father and the love that came with it, the shaping of duty and discipline. She has always missed out on guidance. And the poor baby Keegan, how will he fare?

Anne-Therese opens Colleen's last letter and looks at the photograph inside. Colleen looks worn. Frayed bits of frosty-dyed hair frame her face.

How are you? Getting enough sleep? How is the baby? The photograph you sent was lovely. You and the baby look very healthy.

The photograph shows the three of them. The man looks very much like Colleen's ex-husband, David. Anne-Therese can't decide what more to say. Beautiful things are always being destroyed these days. She puts her pen down and takes in the scene across the street. Children she doesn't recognize pick weeds from the Craiggs' unmowed lawn. It would have upset Anne-Therese's mother, God rest her soul, to behold such a scene. Anne-Therese had always lived with her mother on this street and never once seen a home deserted. The grass is brown with thirst and almost as tall as the children, who have begun to lash each other with the weeds.

Anne-Therese immediately recalls Colleen in the bathroom some twenty years ago, stooped over the enamel sink filled with water. She had been in the backyard for hours, harvesting the dill, raspberries, cucumbers and Sweet William with her sweet grandmother, Anne-Therese's mother.

"I am a Bedouin," Colleen had said. "I haven't had water for 30 days. Have you a ladle?"

Colleen's eyes were glassy, her mouth hung open like a stray dog's on a dead-hot summer's night. "Water," she said. "I will use my hands. Come. Share with me."

By scooping her hands in the water, she drank the basin dry and became Colleen Mainwaring again, aged twelve, Catholic, daughter of Alex and Eva Mainwaring, wearing blue-jean pedal-pushers, North Star runners and speaking like the A-student she was. "Things taste good only when you haven't had them before. I believe in self-deprivation."

Of course she did not know how much she sounded like her grandfather when she spoke about deprivation. He had been dead ten years already and no-one ever talked about him.

I am keeping quite well. The weather is very warm, but I don't
suntan anymore. You should tell your mother not to either. The
sun is much harsher than when she and I were girls.

Your mother should be telling you some things, Anne-
Therese would like to say. If your mother had raised you with
authority and guidance you would know where you belong. If
your father had been a man...But she can't say this—she
knows it's better to be subtle about these things.

Subtlety—that was Eva. Eva: Anne-Therese's sister, and
Colleen's mother. Subtletly, subtlety. That's all Anne-Therese
ever heard coming out her sister's mouth. Especially before
she ran out of their family home, subtly, through the basement
window late one night, and ever-so quietly married Alex
Mainwaring, 23, conscientious-objector, bearded, and on
summer nights, bare-chested, flaunting his smell.

He had a gentle smile and often gave Anne-Therese bear
hugs, whispering, "You'll be all right, Anne-Therese."

She never knew what to say when he said that. What on
God's earth are you talking about? But she didn't ask; she took
the hugs and remembered each one.

Eva Mainwaring subtly announced her marriage by
letter—once she was 3000 miles away. Never to return to the
family home, or to witness their father's manner with their
mother. Never again would Eva stand in the kitchen doorway,
saying, "Well, that's subtle. Well, gee, I don't know if we
understand that you're angry, Pa. Maybe you should really
smash her one to make sure she gets your point." And then,
quietly, "Asshole."

And their mother would be on the floor, her forearm up in
defence, her head down, eyes down, crying, never loudly. She
promised in Ukranian and English that she would make a
better stew next time.

Eva had her way of staying out of control and staying clear
of her father's control. She was the only one in the family to
leave the neighbourhood. She spent her late teens and early
twenties dancing and knew how to drive a car. She took hour-

long baths. She went through jobs like a child eating vegetables, taking a bite here and there, throwing it all away at the slightest bitterness or distaste.

While Anne-Therese worked ten years for the same garment manufacturer, Eva had seventeen different bosses. She lived three provinces away with her husband and children. Eva had no staying-power and neither would her daughter.

Do you remember the Craiggs? You used to play with their eldest child, Martha, when you came to visit. Maureen Craigg died last month, not even a year after her husband passed on. Even in death they didn't part.

Anne-Therese recalled Maureen Craigg and how veiny Maureen's legs were. The Craiggs lived for three generations in that house, invested pride in the garden, the produce— their children. Nothing was left to run wild. But now the kids are either dead or living in different cities across the country. Anne-Therese and Maureen spent many hours on the porch front, stretching in the sun, toes pointed, turning at all angles, flexing their calf muscles at each other. How they compared everything. They touched hands and pressed their fingers together. Anne-Therese's fingers never reached the smooth, long tips of Maureen Craigg's. Sometimes they would keep holding hands, minutes after the comparison was over. Maureen always looked like she never noticed, as if holding hands was an everyday thing. Anne-Therese feigned casualness, too, trying to make herself unaware of their clasp, and thereby making it last longer. They'd soon get onto the subject of children and before Anne-Therese knew it, she was holding her own hand across her chest.

Although Anne-Therese never had children of her own, she took Colleen as her surrogate and talked about her with pride. She did raise Colleen every summer while Eva and Alex vacationed. Colleen was so bright, so much more everything than the Craigg girls.

Remember how little Martha Craigg married her husband because she was pregnant? Remember she left him just after the

81

baby was born? I just received word that after four years of separation, she's gone back to him. I'm so happy for them.

She looks more closely at the photograph Colleen sent. She has always thought Colleen was one gene away from beautiful, that she had the kind of face that could be exquisite or completely hideous with the slightest genetic change. Colleen had always been between extremes. But Anne-Therese never knew which way she would swing. She only hoped.

In her letter, Colleen says that the man is an excellent father to the baby and that she's never beeen happier. She asks, "Why don't you write anymore? Is it because of my divorce?" She doesn't know what to say to this. She puts the letter back in its envelope and tries not to think about it. Clearly, Colleen no longer believes in the self-deprivation she enjoyed as a twelve-year-old over the sink. She must live with the faucets completely open now.

Keegan's a very bald baby. How did that happen? You had a lovely head of hair at birth.

But then she crosses that out. The man's genes must be responsible.

Martha sent a photo of her young family. Her boy has very little hair just like Keegan.

She crosses out those sentences as well—they are a complete lie.

Across the street the adult children of Mr. and Mrs. North get out of a new car. They've moved back home to live with their parents, but not in the way Anne-Therese lived with her mother. These children live at home in order to be supported by their parents, not in order to support them.

The North children are the same age she was when her father called together all six of his children to announce that he had decided Anne-Therese should be the one to tend and manage Mother after he was gone. Anne-Therese would walk Mother to church on Sundays. She was the best-disciplined, he said. She was the one least afraid of duty. For her effort, she would inherit the house. It was unlikely she would marry, he said, since she was 29 already, and no-one had yet asked for her hand.

Anne-Therese had reminded him of her other plans. The line of ladies' suits she had designed and arranged to display at a fashion forum in Montreal later that year. A woman's function, he said, is to serve her husband, and if there is no husband, then she is to obey the father. Her father suggested she talk to Father McKay about her predicament. The Father said she was free to choose between right and wrong, between obedience and selfishness.

I prefer bald babies actually. It makes them seem younger, and so people tend to dote upon them for a little while longer. Babies do love attention.

What she'd like to say to Colleen, in answer to her question, is the truth: no more dreaming. The truth was that Anne-Therese had stopped dreaming *for* Colleen. She no longer imagined possibilities for such a girl. The Theatre, some had predicted: Colleen would land in the centre of the greatest stages in the country. She would become Canada's version of a Broadway Queen. How thirsty she could make herself look. How earnest she could be with a bath towel wrapped around her ten-year-old head, speaking with an Arabic accent.

It had become apparent that Colleen was no different from the rest, that she might not bring the family special recognition, that *People* magazine would not be pounding at the door. Colleen had reached that age when one becomes just like the rest of the relations after all: investing in all the wrong risks; succumbing to the lure of new furniture and dinner parties with the latest china in her cabinet. How the world stops asking about a woman's future once she has arrived at one.

Anne-Therese imagines how it happened for her mother, how she had arrived in Canada 60 years ago and landed a future that offered few choices: married young, pregnant a month later, her belly routinely large with babies and worry.

After Anne-Therese's father had been dead a year, her

mother took off her black dress and wore floral prints until she died. Anne-Therese did not protest. She was glad to be done with the ghostly figure that hovered around the stove, wordless, stuffing cabbage leaves or boiling oats. Anne-Therese welcomed a brighter future for the two of them—with florals and parties, even. But after a day spent watching each other shuffling around the house in slippers neither Anne-Therese nor her mother had energy enough for an evening with guests. The house remained colourful, but still.

Are you in contact with David at all? Easy divorces stop people from working out the rough spots.

She stares at these lines for a long time because she knows they will make Colleen angry. Anne-Therese figures she could teach even the most resistant person a thing or two about duty. She could be a scholar on the subject.

When Anne-Therese was 29 she wanted two weeks off work to take her ladies' suits to the fashion forum in Montreal. Women in the neighbourhood had been buying her designs for years and they all anticipated her fame, even bragging a little when they were the first to buy from her new spring line. Anne-Therese worked hard at fitting each neighbour properly. She often took the bust, waist and hip measurements two or three times, just to make sure she'd sew the perfect fit. How perfectly a woman's curves could complement the embraceable texture of a soft rich wool.

She knew her boss would find a reason to fire her if she took a long holiday, and she could not be as cavalier as Eva was about unemployment. She could not toss off her shoes in Father's direction and tell him to nag someone else. She could not say, "Go bark up another tree," as Eva could. She could not charm her way through a job interview.

She asked for two weeks off, and her boss offered her more. "Take a whole lifetime," he said. She went to the forum with suitcases full of suits and returned home, her bags as heavy as when she left. The lines and the lengths were all wrong, she was told. The materials were second-rate.

She took a job as a bank-teller and learned to enforce the rule of numbers behind a bevelled-glass partition. Juggling dates and debits and credits was easy work compared to the challenge of carving garments from bolts of linen. But more respectable, her father said.

Your grandparents' marriage wasn't built on a bed of roses, but they stayed together for nearly 40 years, you know. Your grandmother had a hard life, but she knew the full love of one man.

And the hate. But such ugliness is not worth retelling, Anne-Therese thinks. Love, love is what's to be remembered. It was love that made him so protective. He always stood in the doorway of the living-room when she or Eva had a visitor. Anne-Therese and Eva played cards on the coffee table and talked politely to the boys, eating Mother's poppy-seed cookies, while Father leaned against the door frame, watching. Then slowly—and without much resistance—his eyes would close. When the alarm he had set earlier in the evening rang, he expected the boys to be gone, and if they weren't, he told them to get their coats on and get the hell out the door.

Eva says they were abused children, but Eva's mind is scorched by the pills she now admits to taking: the anti-depressants and valium. Her version of events cannot be as reliable as those who think clearly. Anne-Therese will never ask her sister the reason for her drug use. She has decided to remain cheerful in letters.

Anne-Therese prefers to say that their father used a strong hand. Yes, he did beat them afterwards, but those were the rules: No boys after 9 PM. He always hit Eva the hardest, and she always managed to be disrespectful, no matter how sore she was.

He only got to hit Anne-Therese once for breaching the nine o'clock rule, and wasn't much interested in the beating. He said it was because she reminded him too much of Mother already, quiet and dutiful, hands clasped, praying in a corner. And anyway, having a girlfriend over past nine o'clock was not the same thing.

When their father died Eva sent a condolence card to their mother, but she didn't go home for the funeral.

Are you getting enough sleep, Colleen? Really? Just try not to do too many things and get your rest. Babies are hard work. You've done so much in your life already, just like your mother. Slow down.

Which reminds her of the announcement Dr. Alan Thompson made during her last visit: "You, Anne-Therese Nadja, are the oldest virgin I've ever examined. Congratulations." Anne-Therese thought she might find pride in this fact, but she has told no-one. If she were to tell Colleen, she knows Colleen would laugh and probably tell the man, and the two of them would sit with the baby in their bed and say, What a deprived old bat. And maybe they would be right.

And maybe they would be wrong. Maybe they would be struck down by God, or the ceiling might strangely cave in on them as they would be laughing together in their unholy bed. Where is her real husband? Where is the man to whom she is truly responsible?

She can feel herself starting to sweat at the thought, her heart beating out of her chest. She wants to lock the door, not let anything in, no more wrongness. She wants to run across the street and find Maureen Craigg alive and say, Maureen, come run with me under the open sun, through a summer field. Come touch my hand with your face.

She holds onto the desk with both hands.

Do what you can and no more. If you don't get a meal on the table one evening, it's not the end of the world. Don't waste your time trying to be exceptional now.

Across the room there is that damned box. She hopes Colleen isn't wasting her moments alone with this kind of rethinking. Trying to reverse the world's problems, like Colleen would, is like telling the sun it must start to rise in the west, she thinks. She keeps trying to think. Her heart is still going.

She decides to put the box to better use as a container for her gardening tools. Knowing your own earth, knowing your place and reaping goodness from it—this is the most valuable thing a person can do. These days, however, her knuckles bother her when she tries to plant or dig. And the earth, it seems, is fighting her. Soil is not soft and compliant in her hands. It does not want her touch.

The box still sits there, asking her to admit that she's been doing it wrong. Everything around her is lashing back, or dying, or not giving thanks, or leaving her with unwanted furniture, with a great-nephew in an ungodly union, with an unmarried niece, with women in the newspaper doing whatever they damned well please with the world and each other and not listening to the order.

She will not burden Colleen with the details. It is her responsibility to be cheerful in letters.

Take care of yourself and Keegan.

Love Aunty Anne-Therese

Anne-Therese starts to address the envelope. Colleen signs her letters from the three of them, but they all have different surnames. The baby's being a rearrangement of letters from Colleen's and the man's surnames. She does not recognize any of them.

Open Zoo

When she takes the small bottle of lemon juice off the super-market shelf instead of the family-sized one, she suspects she might be leaving him soon. Over the last few months, she has been pushing her cart through the aisles, buying small boxes of laundry soap and two-roll packs of toilet paper. She has been thinking David would be on his own soon and wouldn't want the place cluttered with reminders of their sharing.

At home in their apartment she drops her grocery bags on the kitchen floor and leaves them there. The rooms are quiet. Almost everything in them looks mournful, though she enjoys the clutter of old furniture, weary pieces deserted by former tenants of the various places in which she and David have lived since they left high school. In the sunny corner stretches the new sofa David bought with his second paycheque from the law firm. Flagrant, creamy leather with sharp edges, gleaming white, and dishonest as a lottery ticket.

She moves through the kitchen again, checks the chore board posted on the fridge. It's her week to shop and unload the groceries. She heaves the bags from off the floor then shoves soup cans and instant noodle dinners into the cupboards. David is supposed to vacuum and do the laundry this week. Possibly he will do his chores tonight, which, she decides, would be an unfair time to break it to him.

But she imagines telling him anyway: Turn off the Hoover, Honey, I have something I have to say. He would stop vacu-uming, put a hand on his hip and smile. *You want your green sweater washed in cold, right? I already did it.* Her sister Rona's voice enters the daydream: *Don't leave him. He doesn't cheat on you and he washes your clothes for God's sake.* But when she finally says she's leaving him, the look on his face will change into the one she is dreading—his smile drops, and his eyes squint, full of disbelief, as if someone has been run over in front of him.

The eyes on the face she is dreading are always about to cry, and the furrows in his forehead bend into pleading shapes. The lines around his lips move his mouth into those words, *Please don't go.*

She would have to wait. There couldn't be any apology or hesitation in her voice this time. She tried six and a half months ago to leave, but David suggested separate rooms as a solution.

"I'm nearly 30," she said. "I've never lived by myself. I think it's important that I know I can."

"You want to leave a working relationship to be alone and hate it?" David said.

"I've never been with anyone but you," she said.

He said, "Is that what this is all about?" and fanned his arm in the air. "Go on, find out what you're not missing. I won't leave you because of it."

Then she said, "You're my best friend," and started crying. He said, "Exactly, you're mine too." Then he offered to sleep in a different room.

He does not hear the gunfire between them. He does not know there's a war going on.

She decides to cook dinner anyway. The recipe for *tabouli* calls for one-third of a cup of lemon juice, which she pours over soaked bulgur wheat as David comes through the kitchen door wearing his only suit and carrying an Eaton's bag.

His lips taste like banana chips. Once he's finished kissing her, she runs her tongue over her lips and wishes she wanted another kiss. But all she wants is the taste of banana, without the kiss. She licks a spoon dry of lemon juice.

"My dad's coming by tonight. Feeling kind of lonely. You don't mind, do you?"

"He doesn't like *tabouli*," she says.

"Doesn't matter. He'll eat it. Guess what I bought?" He twists his face into a grin and points at the bag.

"I don't know." She tries to make her voice sound playful.

"What do we need more than anything?" He pulls out a four-slice toaster—brand new with the warranty taped on the box. "No more burnt Sundays."

She says, "Right," and thinks of "Three bucks? It's only worth a dollar,"—words he had said ten years ago at the outdoor flea market while bartering for their two-slice toaster, which only browned three sides and usually burnt two of them. She had stood beside him laughing. Her hair was long and thin then, like wisps of fine copper wire. She remembers it flying in the wind against David's shoulder as he bartered. The trees around them—their leaves shuddering and falling in drops of gold and red. Down the back of David's pants her hand massaged as far as it could go. He loved the feel of her fingers sliding under his shorts and pressing on the last vertebrae of his tailbone. He had told her so many times.

He carried a knapsack then, big enough to hold a toaster, text books, groceries and a sleeping-bag. So they stuffed the toaster into his pack and carried it home to their attic suite, fixed tea, made toast and ate in bed the rest of the day.

"Say goodbye to Old Smokey." He unplugs it and places the two-slicer on the floor beside the recyclables bin.

She says, "Don't."

"What?"

She looks down.

"For sentimental reasons?" he asks, smiling.

The thought looks like it pleases him.

"Yeah," she says, but suspects herself of storing the appliance for the day she will move out, in preparation to meet those words of her sister: "Expensive as hell out there on your own, you know." She will be armed with a response: "I have all the appliances I need, Rona. I don't need to buy anything."

"And I bought another dress shirt," he says, unwrapping the plastic from the shirt. "Feel it. One-hundred per cent cotton."

The pinstripes are mauve-coloured, lined in placid rows on a greyish background. "Nice," she says.

"As soon as I'm called to the bar," he says, "I'll be able to afford another suit, too."

"Right," she says, and then a feeling she hopes is courage swells in her. "David?" she says, trying to remain calm, do normal things like chop parsley into a bowl, blending the green flakes carefully together.

He says, "Can it wait a minute? I've got to deal with a few papers."

She can hear the panic setting in. She knows he knows. He does this every time, finds a distraction—a cheque book that needs balancing or a curtain rod that's in sudden need of some glue. One time he suggested they go for a beer. "Mom and Dad never went out when they were still together." And when she agreed to the drink, thinking they would discuss their impending separation over a glass of beer, he insisted on sitting at a table with a built-in video game, and spent the entire evening slamming quarters into slots and pounding buttons.

"David, I need to talk."

"About what?" His face moves into that expression she can't stand even imagining, the one that says, Do anything, but don't leave.

Possibly it is not really his face that she dreads. Sometimes the face more horrible is one from a street corner long ago. The face belongs to a man she's never met but only watched, while her father's voice instructed her, "Look carefully, little girl. That's what's around the corner for you."

She was fourteen at the time and ready to run, aching for a chance at life outside of town, of her neighbourhood, of her house. Dreams full of limitless space, weeds and vines, of morning glory, foxtails and dandelions growing wherever they pleased. She would have room in this place to stretch and run free.

"You run away, and that's the face you'll look at all your life. Filthy old buggers with no morals, thousands of them. You want to kiss those types? That's what happens to the ones that run. Lookie over there—you think she's glamorous? She's just a goddam whore."

She kept her eyes on the man. She watched him touch the breasts of a girl whose hips rubbed against the side of his car.

"I'm showing you this 'cause I care. You've gotta wait for the marrying kind to take you away."

"About what?" David repeated.

"Nothing," she said, "it can wait." She turned instead to the lemon juice and calculated how much of the 225 ml bottle she had used. Two more bowls of *tabouli* and the bottle would be finished.

She lies on the bed, eating. The sound of David's feet shuffling in the kitchen and the scraping noises of her fork on the plate hang static in the bedroom, hers. They had become room-mates this year, except for the occasional kiss and tribute to their sexual past, which had ended its consistency and passion some ten months earlier.

The silence in her bedroom makes her feel as if her throat is clogged. There must be a place to shout. Another house, another city. She doesn't know where. She looks at the phone. The rest of the world is on the other end of it. She picks the phone book up, scans the first pages for long-distance directory assistance and area codes. Anywhere. Dials 1-212-555-1212. The operator says, "Good Evening, New York Telephone," but she doesn't know anyone there and hangs up.

She visualizes herself jumping in the car, driving across the prairies, not knowing where she is headed. A memory rerun of Mary Tyler Moore driving to the Twin Cities in her early-seventies hatchback comes over her, and that theme music: *You might just make it after all.*

She wonders about not making it, not finding a job or a proper apartment, and worries that she will live on the street.

Her fingers dial 1-514-555-1212 to hear: "Bonjour, can I help you?" in heavy French. She likes the sound of it. She says,

"Pardon me?" and lets the operator repeat herself. Then she hangs up.

The phone rings as soon as she puts the receiver down. Her sister Rona's voice is raspy from too many cigarettes, excited because of a job offer in Whitehorse, and full of long sentences about how she will be moving there next month and what she will take. After a long silence Rona says, "Well?"

"I just can't seem to tell him."

"You're just going to have to leave, I guess," Rona says. "Though you know how I feel about the whole thing."

What you need to see is a bruise, she wants to say to Rona. The problem here is that I have nothing to show you. I can't give you a quick-sentence explanation:

He had an affair.
He comes home drunk every night.
He deals cocaine and puts our lives in jeopardy.

All that he's done since we got married is go to bed with two women, but he didn't have intercourse with them, so that doesn't count, right? He comes home drunk once a week, which isn't much I guess. Most of his friends deal hash to supplement their incomes. Why should that concern me?

"Can I come with you?" she asks Rona.

"I don't think you'd like it," Rona says. "Neither would David. There's a lot of darkness in the winter. Dad doesn't think I should go, of course."

"I meant just me, by myself."

"I guess," Rona says. "But you should think very carefully before leaving David."

"Have I ever told you that he tells me to 'fuck off, bitch' when I try to wake him up off the sofa?"

"What?" Rona says.

She repeats herself.

"It's hard to believe."

"It's sort of easy to forget, too. He doesn't even remember doing it. The next morning he gets up early and makes *huevos rancheros* or some other exotic dish for me. Brings breakfast on a tray with a yellow rose in a vase, like something out of a movie. Fresh coffee, too."

But she doesn't believe the breakfast tray is for her. It's for his mother, and he is his father, and she and David are standins, rewriting the wrongs of his parents' marriage. She has known this always. He insists on her staying, but she wonders if it's her he's married to, or if he's in love with the idea of a lasting marriage, one that doesn't end in a courtroom, bitter with children split from their father, the father so lonely.

David comes into her room, smiles, and points at the plate and fork on the floor, "Can I take that?" There's a dishcloth over his shoulder.

She nods, says "Got to go" into the receiver, waits for Rona to say goodbye, and puts the phone down.

"Mind if I sit down here?" he asks, looking at her bed. "How was work today?"

She says, "Go ahead, sit. It was okay."

The bed hardly moves as he crouches on it.

Years before, it would move like a sea and they'd pretend to be stranded on top, taking waves across their water bed, rolling from edge to edge, laughing while stripping thin shirts off each other's backs. His long mane of thick black hair. His lips smoothing across her bare shoulders.

Take off that suit. She wants to say this, but not because she desires his body naked. Take off that suit, and quit reminding me of who I'm not, of how many decisions I haven't made.

"You need a break," he says while his fingers etch their way down her ankle sock. "That's what you want to talk about, isn't it?"

"Yes."

"How about a vacation by yourself? We could borrow the cash."

"That doesn't solve anything," she says, pulling up her sock. "I just want to go." The more room you give, she wants to say, the less room there is that's actually mine. The movement I have is *given* to me, doled out—an open zoo, an illusion of liberty.

"You could take a trip and then apply to a professional program, say. What's another student loan at this point?"

"David, I've got to go for a while," she says, competing for his attention with the door bell ringing.

"That's what I'm saying. I agree."

"I don't know for how long."

"As long as you come back," he says, laughing as he stands. "Duty calls. Got to get the door."

Once he has left the room, she constructs a scenario: her boss in the morning, how she will quit, the letter she will write David, explaining herself perfectly. The clothes and books and trinket things she will miraculously fit into the car.

The room in the shared house she will rent, or the basement suite without windows, or the plot of grass in the park that she'll lay her sleeping-bag on. She watches her scenario collapse into the sound of her father's voice rising: I told you so. And then she foresees the panhandling she'll do, the street walking, cold nights. The life outside that she imagines for herself gets damp and dingy.

Mould grows on the dream of escape.

"Hell of a time parking around here," she can hear her father-in-law say from the kitchen.

"Hi, Randall." She flashes a smile at him from the bedroom door.

With her shoes in hand, she rushes into the kitchen. David is scooping *tabouli* onto three luncheon plates. "I thought we could have toast, too." he says.

"I can't stay, David," she says.

Randall looks at the floor.

"Off for a little drive." She smiles apologetically at David. "I'll leave you two to do some talking."

"Well, have fun," David says.

Randall says, "You modern couples."

"I guess," she says.

David scrapes the *tabouli* off her plate and onto their two plates, building mounds of it.

She watches them not looking at each other for a moment. "Maybe I'll take some of that with me," she says, grabbing a container, heaping some into it.

She opens the fridge, not wanting anything in particular. A big sack of Red Delicious stares out at her from the crisper. She takes the whole bag and then stuffs a block of cheddar into her pocket. She watches her hands claw at containers as if the hands are not hers, as if they are appendages on loan, stashing food for the winter ahead.

David and Randall are quiet. She glances at Randall, catches his look of concern. If she runs now, David won't start hunting her down until Randall has left. She feels David's look on her, but she can't meet his eyes—they'll be flashing a red warning. A stop sign. Danger ahead. For your own safety, stay inside the compound. Do not leap the fence.

She finally looks up and brushes with the face she has been expecting. The eyes. The forehead, wrinkled in the shape she knew it would be. His mouth—about to speak, but silent. Her hands keep on moving. They close the fridge and turn the knob on the front door.

"Hey," David says. "Where's all that food going?"

"Visiting," she says.

He says, "I was going to make Dad an apple crisp for dessert." He forces a broad, easy smile and puts his hand on Randall's shoulder.

"Oh, I see," she says, walking back to the counter. "Here." She lifts apples out of the sack. Then she moves quickly to the door, not wanting a look from either of them. Taking the knob in hand again, she tries to find the momentum and conviction she had only a minute ago.

"That's not enough," David says. "It'll be a pretty flat crisp."

"I don't mind," Randall says. "Let the lady go do her visiting."

"Have all of them," she says. From out of her bag she pulls the apple sack and leaves it against the wall.

"What else do you think you're taking?"

Randall stands and fusses with the lining of his coat pockets.

"You've left me cinnamon and brown sugar, haven't you?" David continues. "You're not taking staples."

"I think I'll use the washroom," Randall says.

"No, Dad," David says.

"Stay, Randall," she says and watches her hand lunge for the front door, which she opens and then closes from the other side, the outside.

She had always planned to take the grand flight of stairs easily—with long, confident steps—but her sense of stride is waning. Maybe tomorrow would be a better day to leave. Her legs keep moving—they persist in taking her down the stairs, closer to the landing, and out of the apartment building.

There is no time to pause, even. She is in her car, starting the engine, not waiting for the right moment or a sense of direction. She accelerates into a line of traffic, thinking only of freeways.

Belongings

David did not notice his old car pull up. He continued to heave boxes marked CAREFUL and OF SENTIMENTAL VALUE from the truck while talking absently with a man whose name he could never remember. He only found it necessary to converse with the man every couple of years, and only when moving furniture for his ex-wife's best friend.

"So, David," the man said. "I hear you're living in the City Hall area."

"Nearby, I guess," David said. Although the man wasn't entirely accurate about the district, David and his fiancée *had* recently moved.

"Well, congratulations on your son," the man said, lifting GRANNY'S CHINA. "He's beautiful. We've got the picture you sent on our mantel."

David did not have a son and for a moment he didn't understand why the man thought he did. "You must be talking about Colleen." His ex-wife. "She has a kid now."

She had failed twice at leaving him. The day she succeeded was the same day David was called to the Bar.

On a clear afternoon in the late fall David had received the news regarding his employment future. Carrying his job offer in hand, he had left the office in a celebratory mood, walked smack into the cool air (still earning an articling student's wage, without money for a winter coat), jumped a bus, got off at the Government Liquor Store, bought a bottle of Mumms and a newspaper announcing the fall of the Berlin Wall. He stuck his thumb into traffic, knowing it would be the last time he would hitchhike, having become, in one short day, legitimate: employed, with prospects of a bank balance. He was no longer bound to a fierce little budget that relied heavily on Visa cash advances.

He walked home with brisk strides. He approached the gate to his basement apartment and noticed Colleen standing outside the door, holding her stomach. He raised the brown bag into the air and cheered, "I made it," forcibly ignoring, he knew, her nervous stomach, not wanting her to unload another doubt.

He moved closer, kissed her hard on the lips. He wanted to say, Don't wreck this for me, but, by saying nothing, she already had.

Before they could enjoy the bottle together, she packed a bag of food and left for good.

The man quickly passed David a box of shoes and boots. By the look of embarrassed sympathy on the man's face, David knew the man was now recollecting the bits of gossip he had heard, piecing together the story of his separation. The details of his life had undoubtedly circulated around the coffee-tables of many people he barely knew.

"God, sorry," the man said. "I just can't keep up."

David said, "Neither can I." He held the box. "I can carry more," he said.

The man passed him PHOTO ALBUMS: PRECIOUS.

Colleen got out of the car, slammed shut the rusted door and balanced on her shoulder four pizza boxes and a thin package wrapped in Santa heads. She approached the moving truck with confidence, nodded at the man, then at David, whom she hadn't seen in two months.

The sky was as cloudless as the day she had left him crying in the doorway of their apartment. The grass and the dying geraniums in planters were the same brown as a year ago. Even the evergreens seemed to conspire to remind her.

"I got your favourite, David," she said, huddling the boxes under her coat, rushing into the house, breathless by the time she reached the top of the stairs. She stood on the landing, chewed a hangnail momentarily, and wished she could give up her old habit of buying for David's tastes. She consoled herself by recalling an article she had recently read, entitled

"Finishing Him," in which a therapist said it takes two years to "complete" a failed relationship. It had only been one year since she had walked out.

She stumbled through the kitchen, avoiding appliances lying on their backs, electrical cords extending everywhere, half-hung curtains. She stumbled over a teapot on the floor and sent it careening to the wall, smashingly, but it did not break.

She slid the pizza boxes into the oven and searched the house for Joy, trying to block from her view the room she had once called The *Joy of Sex* Den. She wanted to forget that the room had ever existed for her, that she and David, as teenagers, had performed The Book, page by page, contorting their bodies into every illustrated position.

Colleen found Joy farther down the hall, stretching on a thin beam of winter light that moved across the mattress in Joy's parents' bedroom. Except for the loud whitish sunlight that glared from every window, the house was quiet. Joy's great hair fanned out above her head, wispy twine-coloured strands spreading madly over the bed of large blue roses. Joy's parents had vacated the entire house that day for a rented apartment, which would give Joy and her two kids, and her husband—if he were to come back, and she were to let him— a clean house in a secure neighbourhood, rent free.

"I'm going to change the wallpaper in here," Joy said, smiling at the freshly washed carpet, at the garbage bags marked UNDERTHINGS. "And the drapes," she added.

"You look well," Colleen said, carefully. "Really."

Joy smiled wider.

The smile was closed-lipped and knowing, and it protected Joy from questions she might not want to answer. The smile reminded Colleen of the many afternoons they had been together as Husband and Wife. Colleen had always played the Husband, trying to remove Joy's nightie, first caressing her shoulders, then kissing her neck, and Joy was the Wife, giving her mother's satisfied closed-lipped smile, quick to squirm and roll over, saying, "Not tonight, honey."

"Remember how we'd swing from those drapes playing Jungle," Joy said. She brushed her finger along the fringe of the drapes, then crunched a handful of the heavy floral material into a ball and buried her nose in it. "I love the smell of old dust."

"Don't you want to talk about it?" Colleen asked.

"No," Joy said. She tipped over a hefty bag and poured white bras, lacy silks and flannel nighties onto the mattress. She sorted them with great concentration, her eyes not moving from the garish blue roses climbing all over the bed.

Colleen wanted to grab her and say she would have no trouble meeting someone else, but Joy started to sing. She wanted the subject changed.

"Husband and Wife" or "The Affair"—Joy said she could hardly remember either. But Colleen thought of their kisses vividly and regularly. Ten-year-old Joy played an obliging Mistress, taking off her nightie, wrapping her legs around Colleen, saying, "Darling, take me." But Joy really preferred to play the Husband coming home from work, unlocking his front door, walking in the house to find his Wife (Colleen) in bed, her hair tousled, and accuse her of wrongdoing. Joy loved to howl, "How could you do this to me?"

Affairs had shaped both their marriages, Colleen had decided. Joy had discovered her own husband on top of their babysitter last month. And Colleen imagined David was in the kitchen now avoiding her, no longer her husband, because of the many games that had been played. She had low expectations of Husband and Wife, and a desire for The Affair, with its promise of passionate legs and nighties on the floor.

If Colleen hadn't become proficient, as a ten-year-old, at scripting love scenes, she wonders if she would have approached Carl two years ago with the expectation of a similar kind of excitement. Would she have talked to Carl after class at the university, explaining how much more interesting he was than the instructor? Would she have invited him to the student pub, confessed her marital problems, found his blue eyes so deep, his compassion overwhelming?

Would she and Carl have a child today had she not played The Affair? She worried that her life was entirely arbitrary.

David came into the room as soon as she thought of him. A slice of pizza in one hand, a string of long white cheese hanging from his beard.

"Thanks for the *prosciutto*," he said to Colleen. His long back stretched cold and thin in the doorway. She thought of him naked suddenly, how his shoulder-blades jutted out so harshly.

Colleen said, "Wait," and handed David the package wrapped in Santa heads. "Here. Merry Christmas."

David made no move to take it. It was the first Christmas they had spent apart in eleven years.

"Can't I still give you a gift?"

"I have nowhere to put it," David said.

The gift was a piece of cardboard cut into the shape of a cat. The manufacturer's packaging read "Flat Cat—the ideal low maintenance pet." Colleen had not meant to buy it. She had only been walking Robson Street last week for the effect the sidewalk had on her baby. The sloped curbs and broken pavement lulled him to sleep, so she pushed him in the buggy up and down the length of a block where the Flat Cat had stared out at her from a shop window. The words Low Maintenance drew her into the store.

There are two kinds of women, David had often quipped, high and low maintenance. He had always said Colleen was the former. She asked why he didn't leave her then, and David would always say that wasn't his point.

David took the gift under his arm. "Tara's coming to pick me up. I can put it in her car." When he looked at Colleen standing there, he felt himself smile, pleased that she no longer lived with him, relieved that he would not be going home with her tonight. He would never again have to listen to her schemes—her plans to take exotic vacations on credit, borrowed time and money. How she thrived on complete uncertainty.

She often said she'd rather die than know how she was going to spend the next week.

Colleen said. "Right, there you go, Tara's car will do," and returned him to another time. Off went the beard, glasses and Rockports and on went the frayed jeans, Dayton boots and a mop of ratty black hair.

He had smoked himself brainless in his late teens, the late seventies, introduced to Colleen (a girl from a cloistered neighbourhood—there was a Catholic Nunnery on the corner of her street) a subtle variety of hangovers, and given her the ability to identify pot plants from regular house plants at a glance. Together she and David spent many evenings together in anyone's basement, carousing with friends, most of whom had since ended up in jail or had completely reformed themselves into church-going family people. After such an evening, Colleen and David would drive to the beach, take a blanket to the sand and dream their future together. He vigorously, she with hesitance. He had decided on the year they would buy a house, the month they would have their first child, the kind of modest vacation they should take.

She asked, "What would you do if I died tomorrow?"

"I'd be sad for a long time," David said. He puffed on a cigarette with great solemnity. "But I'd meet someone else and get married. But don't worry, you won't die."

When he spoke this way she wanted to kill him. He was too certain of their common fate. She did not want a bit part in her own life. If she wasn't there to fill the role he'd scripted, a faceless Colleen-substitute was ready to advance at any moment.

Colleen knew Tara was allergic to cats. She was not the perfect substitute. Unlike Colleen, Tara could not fill a bowl with Salmon Delight, empty a litter box, hold a cat on her lap or even share the same air with one. Tara had an especially violent reaction to the short-haired cat David had bought near the end of his relationship with Colleen in an attempt to fill the gap, the space growing between them. The cat was their child, their trial run at having a baby.

The tabby Gigi had a double-barrelled surname, her own dishes, her own bedding and medical appointments. Colleen and David took her for her shots together, nervous first-time parents, their eyes filling.

"I'm going to get another slice," David said. "Good deal you've got here, Joy. Your parents are amazing." He left the room shaking his head. Colleen looked malnourished and green, he thought. He had heard her mumble something about breast-feeding sapping all her energy and how she still got up five times a night. He had never seen her baby. He could not imagine him.

He walked into the kitchen and took the last slice of pizza from the last box.

Joy said, "This is my bedroom now. I'm going to be sleeping over the spot where I was conceived. A little too close to home, isn't it?"

Colleen looked at the green plastic bags in mounds through-out the terribly square room. "Where are the hangers?"

"But then again," Joy said, "how could I afford to turn down Mom's offer? Free rent, a chance to save for a down-payment. I have to admit it's nice finally to be safe like my mother was, safe from choices." Joy stood in front of the mirror and wrapped her hair into a puffy, loose bun—a flattish bouffant.

"Even when I was a kid and that insurance agent was hanging around, wanting to take Mom away for the weekend to Reno, she said she didn't have a choice. She was married, simple as that."

Like David, Joy, too, had recently become someone else. Having two small children and an absent husband helped speed her metamorphosis. Her days were no longer new, and there were no beginnings anymore, only extensions. She was finally the age she had always wanted to be. Ten years earlier she had let Colleen drag her into nightclubs and discotheques, engaging in perfunctory rituals of what she thought it meant to be twenty. But Joy had really been waiting her whole life to be 30, and looked to 40 as a place of comfort, warm memories, a savings account, toting armchairs to the beach, sitting in the shade, and not being obliged by youth and vigour to lie on gritty sand under the full hot sun.

Colleen suspected Joy would always wear a nightgown to bed now.

Colleen's attention turned to David eating ravenously in the kitchen. She watched him take more than his share of garlic toast with his pizza. The other men leaned against shiny appliances and drank beer from cans.

Before Colleen could imagine something about David, pretend to know about his new life, the trouble he may be in, the overeating he may be doing, she heard the men's voices soften as a clip-clip of heels grew in their direction.

David watched his fiancée walk across the hardwood floor toward him. She strode in the low-heeled pumps he had bought her. The shoes had, for a decorative reason, metal taps on the heels and toes that effectively announced her arrival. Her long strides and proud head were lawyerly, he thought, and befitted her new position as a Prosecutor for the Crown.

He was glad for her tactical approach: bowl them over with confidence. For Tara to appear in the same house as Colleen and Joy, a plan had been required, David thought. He had told Tara everything. About the teen sex den in the house, how he and Colleen had been in love for at least half of their relationship, how two weeks before she walked out, he and Colleen had bought *What Shall We Name the Baby* at a garage sale and pretended they were expecting. He was always honest.

"My wife left me for another man who impregnated her six weeks later." He said it on their first date.

Tara, too, had been left.

"What's she doing here?" Joy asked Colleen.

Joy had never expected Tara to arrive. She had never anticipated Tara's or Carl's existence. When Joy walked down the aisle behind Colleen, carrying the train, she had thought marriage would preserve Colleen in a kind of stillness. That the marriage would make the future, sealed air-tight by vows, less likely to spoil.

Vows should be preserved. She had said this to her husband last month, but by then he had already broken their world. She had to preserve what was left, and carry each wanted, salvageable piece of that life into the new house, this new life alone with her kids. Continuity had to remain. The bastard.

"She's picking up David," Colleen said. "That's why she's here."

Joy watched Tara briefly, the way her tar-black hair framed her face, accentuating her high cheeks, thick red lips and blemishes. She wore no cover-up. She did not look like anyone's second choice.

Tara latched her finger through David's belt loop and laughed. "Some old guy across the street wouldn't let me park in front of his house," Tara said. "He said it was his spot. I told him curbs were municipal property. He said I had better move on."

"Old Andrews got her," Colleen laughed.

"He sweeps the sidewalk everyday, you know," Joy said.

"He's parked there for 30 years."

"What an old fool," Colleen said.

Joy said, "Maybe not." In her teens she had called him an intrusive old grunt. Today he was, in her mind, a man of pride and simplicity. One who kept his promises, one who said "I do" and meant it. He knew what he expected of each day. His world did not spin.

David stopped laughing before he wanted to. He wanted to engage with his wife-to-be, to hold her proudly, to say, I am glad for all that has happened, that Colleen finally did leave me so that Tara could come into my life. He wanted to announce these things to everyone. But then Carl arrived.

Carl and the damned baby appeared in the doorway before he had a chance. The baby, of course, supplanted Tara as the highlight of the room. The baby kicked and gurgled and waved his arms and the moving men reacted:

"What a live-wire."

"Those backpacks saved me and my wife."

"Big boy, that's for sure."

The baby sat in the pack innocently, smiling toothless at everyone—especially David, it seemed.

He said, "Friendly creature," and put the last crust of toast into his mouth. He felt Tara let go of his belt loop and say she just remembered something in the car. He asked her to take the package wrapped in Santa heads.

She walked away as briskly as she had arrived. As soon as David heard her shoes clipping down the stairs, he felt Carl lean toward him.

"So," Carl said. "I hear you're going to tie the knot a little tighter this time."

Joy started to clap and her eyes brightened. She looked past Carl, directly behind him and laughed. "This old man, he played one, he played nic-nac on my thumb," she said to the baby. She hummed what she couldn't seem to remember.

David knew a great deal about Carl, and he hoped this might work to his advantage one day. He knew that Carl was a penniless student who didn't believe in marriage or in other ways of silencing women's histories. He knew Carl insisted his son have Colleen's surname. He knew Carl had a fear of traditions.

"Well, at least I'm not afraid to tie one," David said, finally. The last time he had spoken with Carl was at the signing of his divorce papers.

Joy said, "This old man, he played three, he played nic-nac on my knee."

At the time of the divorce, David had been articling downtown in a prestigious office, panelled in aged oak, and opulent with its select view of the city's harbour. In an uncharacteristic moment, he had offered his legal services to Colleen, making himself the Husband, the defendant's lawyer and the respondent's lawyer, all at once.

He endured an hour of watching his wife and her lover grin over his legalese: since the celebration of the marriage, the Respondent has committed adultery with Carl Richard Eyre on various and divers occasions...

"You're right," Carl said, relieving his baby son of his winter wrappings. "I am afraid of the courts in my bedroom."

Colleen walked into the kitchen before David could think up a response. Joy's singing ploughed into his thoughts, and he pushed the old man, now playing nic-nac in heaven, away.

He watched Colleen take Carl and the baby between her arms. He watched Carl struggle to remove the baby's hat.

Once the hat was off, he stared at the baby's flesh and skull and eyes like hers. The child was not a phantom after all, appearing only in photographs and phone conversations.

If it were his child, he wondered if the eyes would be that shape? If Colleen's genes would have been dominant? Would their baby have had teeth by now? Would it be drooling all over Colleen's hand today? Would she be teaching the child to say Dada?

He had an excuse to leave the kitchen. The other men had moved to the living-room, and he did not want to be separated from them.

From across the kitchen, Joy yelled, "Hey, Carl, how about helping me clean this freezer out while Colleen feeds the little one?" She did not want him to follow David into the living-room. She didn't want him to help the other men with the moving. She didn't want him in her house, really, for fear that he would take it apart or deconstruct it. He reminded her of the insurance man who used to come calling for her mother. He, too, wouldn't leave well enough alone.

She thought Carl's belief about marriage being an oppressive institution was ridiculous, and an affront to her life. Would he find something inherently problematic in maintaining old friendships, too? If she were to let him into her living-room, would he critique the books in her boxes? Would he say that her life was fraught with the wrong kind of literature and weak ideas? She preferred not to know.

Colleen carried her baby into the unpacked dining-area and negotiated her way among the boxes, bags of cushions, stacked chairs and table legs with their feet splayed into the air. She sat in privacy among the teetering boxes and manipulated her nipple into the baby's mouth. She became absorbed by the split of her selves, these people together, their various demands, the different eras of her life, now merging into something she didn't understand. She felt fragmented but whole, like a completed puzzle.

She watched Tara return to David's side in the living-room, with a sleek leather jacket and Bolero across her arm.

Tara raised her voice at Colleen. "We have a carpet in our

place that used to be yours. We're going to throw it out unless you want it."

"We mean, could you use it?" David said. "Could you come by our place and get it?"

Before Colleen could answer, Carl came out of the kitchen and announced they definitely could use such an item.

Their apartment, however, was fully carpeted.

"I thought you'd want to see his apartment, his apartment with her," Carl explained to Colleen as they stood at David and Tara's front door. Carl held a soother in the baby's mouth. Colleen put her fist to the door.

"Let's get it over with," she said, and dropped her hand against the door, until Tara answered.

Tara's earrings: a table on one lobe, a chair on the other. Colleen didn't need to see the rest of the place. She imagined a solid domesticity of sturdy furniture and functional artwork. But when she stepped into the hallway, she saw herself all over the apartment—her handwriting on spice jars, the pewter mug she gave David on his twenty-first birthday, the lamp they had received as a wedding present eight years ago, now wearing a new shade.

"We've got a party to get ready for," Tara said. "I've got to do my hair if you…"—her voice trailed into the bathroom.

David said, "The carpet doesn't fit where we'd planned to use it."

"I'm sure we'll find a spot for it," Colleen said, suddenly aware of her excruciatingly cheerful voice, of the Saturdays she had wasted buying carpets, of all her planning for a home that would never be. Her and David's attempt at drawing a family tree, pulling lines together from each of their parents to themselves, imagining lines extending into someone not yet born, never would be.

Carl and her dozing baby moved around the apartment,

together. She wondered how she would explain this world to her son.

Photographs stood erect and forceful on the mantlepiece— David and Tara with grandparents, the new couple holding someone's baby, the new couple in each other's arms, wrapped in ski wear. The photographs worked like cue cards, she imagined, visual prompts to remind them of who they were, now, who each of them loved.

The view from the large window in the living-room exposed a street full of apartment blocks. There were few trees in the immediate vicinity and the ones there looked gangly and young, without majesty. There was no beauty here, Colleen thought.

Tara stepped out of the bathroom and followed Carl throughout his circuit of the apartment, watching him as he picked up the photographs. She behaved with suspicion, as if he might steal something from her, as if he were capable of taking the happiness out of this marriage, too.

"You're welcome to go through those boxes," Tara said, pointing to the floor.

Colleen's casserole dishes and old wedding-present crystal vases were stacked in boxes in a corner.

"Right," Colleen said, and crouched over the dishes.

David watched her on the floor, on her knees, sifting through his junk. "That lovely glass salad bowl was given to Tara at a shower last weekend," he said. "It's off to the Sally Ann if you can't use it."

"This is my cheese plate." Colleen held up a slab of marble.

"It's crap, Colleen."

She didn't look up. "Well, I don't know if I'd say that."

"It's crap," he said again. He enjoyed telling her this, suddenly enjoyed her on her knees, savoured her poverty with Carl. He wanted to yell it at her, "It's crap." The whole deal's crap, he wanted to say.

Colleen pulled a knife out of a box. She said, "I was wondering what happened to my knives. I've been chopping with K-Tel lately."

Tara said, "Take everything."

There was a capsule of Joy's mother's bath oil on the tub's edge. It was an imposition, a forced entry, but Joy wanted it. The oil as heirloom, something to soak in and absorb, her mother's life. Joy took herself gently into the bath and washed off the residue from the long moving day. Everything was perfect and in its place. Nothing had broken in the move. She would be all right.

She would trace the groove her mother had made until she was comfortably settled. She would hold her breath, hold herself beneath the foamy surface. Her head would rest against the enamelled finish of the tub, legs drawn up, embryonic, until every inch of skin was safe from the cool air above.